Publisher's note: This is another of Martin Archer's exciting and action packed novels in *The Company of Archers* saga. It is the story a serf who rose to become the captain of what was left of a company of crusading English archers—and what happened to him and his men after he led the survivors of his company back to the dangerous and brutal land of medieval England. The first book in this saga is entitled *The Archers.*

PREFACE

Taking a mail train full of currency or capturing a Spanish treasure ship is nothing compared to what were surely the greatest thefts in history— when the captain of a company of English archers and his men systematically stole the entire treasury and the religious relics of the world's greatest and richest empire, and escaped to Cornwall with their galleys full of chests of gold and priceless relics. This is part of the on-going story of how it all began and what happened when he tried to turn the relics into coins for himself and his company. Today's men would have done quite well in Britain's dangerous medieval times. *The Company of English Archers.*

Book Five

The Hostage Archers

Chapter One

Fighting on two fronts.

My brother, William, was in Cornwall with the archers and preparing to fight off Lord Cornell's efforts to take the Cornwall lands where we train our archers; I was in Derbyshire with a company of mercenaries, every one of them a wondering Scot, to lay a siege on Cornell's keep. We were here to prevent reinforcements from being sent to Cornell and, hopefully, bring him and his men back to relieve the siege.

We'd only been at it for a couple of weeks but, even so, our siege seemed to be going well with no serious losses on either side. Our only casualty so far was one of Scots who took a crossbow quarrel in the shoulder. The damn fool got too close to the ramparts on the outer wall.

Hopefully, the fool's shoulder won't turn black and begin to smell. We're bleeding him and covering him with garlic in order to fight off the poxes.

We've been expecting some sort of a sortie by the castle's defenders ever since we arrived, but so far there has been nothing. Not even a whisper. Cornell has undoubtedly taken most of his men and mercenaries to Cornwall and left only a skeleton force of guards to hold his castle, not enough to come out and fight us in an attempt to break our siege. Unfortunately for us, a small force of men is more than enough to hold Hathersage — because it's a strong keep with a moat, high stone walls with battlements, and a gatehouse with ramparts and archer slits. What is particularly unfortunate about Cornell only leaving a few men to guard his castle is it means it's going to take his men and their families longer to eat up the castle's food reserves and be starved into surrendering.

We, of course, are not about to launch a direct attack against such a strong fortress. It would be suicidal. It would also be quite foolish because the attack would almost certainly fail and the resulting losses turn Captain Leslie and his company of Scots against us.

****** *Thomas*

When we first arrived, we found the village and the mill on the stream next to Cornell's castle deserted and the fields around it empty of sheep. The wooden shutters on the village houses were shut and their doors left unbarred so they wouldn't have to be broken down for someone to enter. Cornell's villagers obviously hope to return.

Most tellingly, there were no animals about when we arrived except for quite a number of very hungry dogs and some cats and a handful of stray chickens, which proved to be quite delicious. The villagers had obviously either moved into the castle with their pigs and sheep or herded them off to more distant fields.

The only thing we knew for certain was that the villagers left in a hurry and intend to return when we are gone—every hovel had at least one spinning wheel or a weaver's loom and many of them still had their owners' wooden plates and bowls. What was missing from almost every hovel in the village was its bedding and food supplies. There wasn't so much as a sack of corn or flour to be found and every root cellar was empty.

Not having the villagers' food to eat was a problem because it meant we'd have to send out foraging parties to buy or steal some from the more distant villages beyond Cornell's lands and manors. It was also a problem if the villagers and their livestock and corn were in the castle because it meant the castle would have a bigger defensive force and more supplies. They'd be able to hold out longer before we can starve them out.

I think the villagers and their livestock are in the castle bailey because of all the stray dogs — they'd be helping herd the sheep and cattle if the manor's livestock had been moved to distant fields; that they've been left to fend for themselves in the village strongly suggests the livestock have been moved into the castle where the dogs would merely be useless mouths to feed.

We may be here a long time so how we would supply ourselves with food was an easy decision to make — we'll buy our food and ale, not just take it. If we buy our corn and meat with good coins, food will come in to us from the villages beyond Cornell's lands; if we try to take the food without paying for it, it will surely be hidden away — and without food we'll be forced to end our siege before can we starve out Cornell's people.

Even worse, our foraging parties might mistakenly take sheep and cattle belonging to a neighbouring lord and cause him to rise up against us instead of staying away in lordly disdain because he's like the King—he doesn't really care who wins so long as he's not bothered.

Fortunately, I'd been able to buy some corn and such along the way and we'd arrived here with a substantial flock of sheep, a couple of wains full of sacks of corn, and half a dozen beeves the Scots' women can slaughter whenever we want the mercenaries to eat beef.

In reality, both the mercenaries I've hired and Cornell's people in the castle are waiting to see what happens in Cornwall. If Cornell wins or worries about losing his keep, he'll almost certainly bring his men back to Derbyshire to relieve our siege; if William and the archers win in Cornwall, on the other hand, the siege here at Hathersage will continue until either Cornell and his survivors return and try to drive us away or the castle's defenders are starved out and surrender.

There are various other possibilities, of course. The worst would be if the local lords raised a force to assist Cornell and tried to lift the siege. William and I don't think it likely because Cornell owes his liege directly to the King who sold him the Cornwall earldom. If anything, the local lords will want Cornell dead and gone so they can try to get his lands and serfs for themselves.

Cornell's vassalage direct to the King was important, of course. It meant the shire's other lords had nothing to gain except casualties if they fight for us or against us. Besides, they probably know of the King's decision to let "God's will" determine the outcome and would not want to risk the King's or God's displeasure by involving themselves in a decision which God alone will make — with our assistance, of course.

The most worrisome possibility of all is that there will be no clear winner to the fighting in Cornwall such that Cornell abandons his efforts in Cornwall and returns to Derbyshire with a force strong enough to defeat us and lift the siege.

If Cornell returns to Derbyshire to relieve the siege, William will have to decide whether or not to follow him back here with our archers and bring him to battle even if it means fighting him on ground that is neither known nor favourable.

I rather suspect William would follow him because our basic problem is the same as Cornell's — neither of us can afford to let the other remain alive and neither of us can afford to let the other possess strongholds from which he can rebuild his forces and start again. Whether we like it or not, we've gotten ourselves into a war that will go on until either Cornell or William are dead — and all their heirs such as my nephew George along with them.

Our reality, however, is different from Cornell's and much more pressing — we need to settle the matter as soon as possible so our archers can embark for the Holy Land and once again start earning their pay by carrying refugees to safety on our galleys and taking Moorish prizes. As it stands, our men have to be paid as often as every year and we can't risk sending them off to earn the coins we'll need to pay them until Cornell and his heirs are dead.

Actually, we wouldn't have a problem paying our men even if the archers stayed in England for many years — no one knows it, of course, but we've a king's ransom in coins in the chests at Restormel and another hoard almost as large in the fortified Cyprus farmhouse we bought and strengthened on our way back to England.

The good news, of course, is there apparently has been some kind of battle in Cornwall and Cornell may already be dead. At least, his death was the rumour which reached us last week and swept through the ranks of Leslie's Scots like a wildfire.

Hopefully, it's true about Cornell being dead. In the meantime, life here was going on here in

Derbyshire as if he is still alive; our siege continues, and Leslie's mercenaries and their families have taken advantage of the empty village and moved into the villagers' empty hovels.

Even more important, the Scots seem quite content with the way things are going—and that's always significant when dealing with mercenaries. Their contentment would change, of course, if their company started taking heavy casualties or they ran out of the corn they need to make bread and brew ale.

****** *Thomas*

Robert Leslie, the captain of our band of Scottish mercenaries, and I were sitting together on a log bench in front one of the village hovels and speculating once again about how long Hathersage would be able to hold out. An old dog had come up to me and flopped over on his side at my feet. This was probably his home, so I scratched him with my sandal and looked at the strange kink in his tail. There was a feel of rain in the air.

Leslie was interested in hearing about my brother William. He wanted to know how someone started out as a serf and got to be the Earl of Cornwall, and why I am helping him if Cornwall is so poor.

I didn't tell him all the many details including the fact I'm William's older brother. What I did tell him was about William being both a very dangerous man to try to cheat or cross and a smart man who supports my plan to establish a school for putting the learning on young British lads as the Greeks and Romans once did on theirs.

"William spent years crusading in the Holy Land as I did myself," I told Leslie. "He knows how hard it is to find dependable men who can scribe and sum enough to work with the merchants and churchmen and lords the archers have to deal with."

I tried to explain why William wants his son George, and the likely lads we've found to study with George, to learn scribing and summing and how to gobble in church talk.

"So they can take over from us when they grow up and we're too old to sail from port to port sorting out problems and seizing coins and prizes."

The dozen or so boys who were my students, I tried to explain to Leslie, were likely lads and not a one of them was from the gentry and accustomed to being given everything without having to fight for it—so it was a great opportunity for them to advance themselves.

We want George and my lads to lead our

company of sailors and archers in the years ahead, don't you see? But he didn't, of course.

Leslie didn't get it. I could see from the look on his face that he didn't understand why George and the boys were being learnt to scribe and sum and gabble Latin and he wasn't interested. He was just trying to be friendly and make conversation. So I stopped trying to explain, and we just sat quietly for a few minutes looking at the walls of the keep his men have surrounded.

After a while, at Leslie's request, I once again began regaling him with a description of my encounter with Cornell's Belgian mercenaries in Sarum when they were on their way to join Cornell in Devon prior to marching on Cornwall.

Mercenaries are something Leslie can understand. And as you might imagine, we both began speculating and laughing about what might have happened in the city that night and how the mercenaries from Flanders might have acted towards the women of the city and responded to being gulled out of their weapons because I told them they couldn't carry weapons into the city on the one day of the year when all the drinks and all the women were free.

Kerfluffle and his men believed me because I'd paid them their "bonus coins from Cornell" just in time for them to go into Sarum on "the day the women and drinks were free."

Those coins and the coins I prepaid Sarum's six alewives for the mercenaries' unlimited "free drinks in honour of St. Epher's Day," were well worth it, even if they did all get roaring drunk and ended up burning down half the city.

Leslie knew all about his fellow mercenary captain and had even served with him in the same army a few years ago. They had served together, he'd already told me two or three times, when they had both contracted for their mercenary companies to fight for old King Henry in one of his campaigns against the Capetian king in Paris.

"He'll never live it down," Leslie roared as he slapped his leg in delight. He'd already heard the story three or four times and still couldn't get enough of it.

We were both still smiling and chuckling at the misfortunes of the Belgian captain and his men when three heavily armed archers rode in from London with a parchment from my brother. The winds and conditions in the channel had been favourable and it had only taken them a little more than two weeks to reach us — and the news they brought was good news, very good news.

We always send two or three men with our

parchment messages. The roads are much too dangerous for a single rider.

Cornell was indeed killed at the battle at the River Tamar ford, George and my students are doing well, and William wants me to return to Cornwall as quickly as possible. *He obviously wants to take our galleys and men back to Cyprus.*

But there was something new — William wants to add Cornell's keep and lands to our holdings as soon as they are taken. He said he thinks we'll have a strong claim to it as the "Will of God" — but only if we have it very firmly in our possession so the King or one of the local lords can't seize it without a fight.

Well, he's right about that, of course; we might be able to hold Hathersage if we have it in our possession. But why does he want it?

****** *Thomas*

Our siege lines have been tight. The people in the castle probably didn't even know their lord is dead. Well, it was Cornell's idea to combine his good Derbyshire lands with the poor lands of Cornwall and now it's likely going to happen — for the Company of Archers and for my brother and my dear nephew George.

According to William's parchment, before I

return to Cornwall, William wants me to consider Leslie or one of the local gentry as a possible vassal to hold Cornell's lands for us — and he wants them held under the conditions of vassalage he'd listed on his parchment message plus any more I think appropriate.   I'm also to scribe the necessary parchments and send them to the King for his approval of "God's will."

William's wanting to hold on to Cornell's castle surprised me because it is so far from Cornwall. On the other hand, Cornell also wanted them both so there's probably something I don't know. I can understand why Cornell wanted the title of earl so he would have a higher precedence when he was prancing around with the gentry at Richard's court; but I don't understand why William wants Cornell's Hathersage — surely he doesn't want our archers to live and train in Derbyshire and for him and George to piss their time away at court when there are things to do and coins to earn?

In any event, it is up to me to make the final decision about Cornell's keep and his lands. If I think Leslie is capable of holding them for us, and he agrees to do so, I'm to write up a contract of vassalage and feoffment on one of the blank parchments William's messenger brought to me in his pouch.

I can tell William's serious about this; he included

a skin pouch full of finely ground charcoal for me to use as ink and some goose feathers I can sharpen to use for quills.

If Leslie makes his mark on the parchment I scribe, I'm to preside over a commendation ceremony wherein Robert Leslie and his mercenaries offer their homage to William, Earl of Cornwall, and become his vassals — and, in return, Leslie and his heirs are granted the honour of holding the Hathersage fief and its lands for us.

On the other hand, if I think Leslie is not up to holding the keep for us or he won't make his mark on our terms or I think he won't honour them, William wants me to stay in Derbyshire until I can find someone else who will.

Well, it's up to me to decide, isn't it? And it's an easy decision to make. I'm anxious to get back to George and the boys so it doesn't take any time at all to reach a decision — besides, the Leslies are our only alternative. Otherwise, good riddance to the place no matter what my brother thinks; these lands are too good and too close to the King and his court — someone will always be trying to get them off us and the King will always be levying taxes and scutages on them for his wars.

After reading William's parchment several times, I invited Leslie and his son to sit with me to hear the latest news from Cornwall. The Scots and their women had seen the messengers arrive and the Leslies and everyone else were quite curious — they'd been anxiously hovering nearby ever since the messengers arrived and handed me the pouch. When I waved they quickly came over and joined me under the wagon where I've been sitting to keep the rain from spoiling the ink on the parchment I'd been reading.

When the Leslies were seated, I gave them my best and warmest big smile and read them the good news — the rumour we heard last week is true — Cornell is dead. Then I began casually and carefully inquiring about their possible interest in staying here and having the honour of holding Cornell's keep as vassals of the Earl of Cornwall, explaining that with Cornell's death his keep and lands were now William's by the Will of God and the King's approval. *Well, I think they are if we can hold them and we sweeten the King and his chancellor as William suggests.*

Their eyes lit up at the thought, as I was certain they would — being as they are poor landless Scots and no coins are required up front — and we began discussing what would be required of someone who wanted to hold Cornell's keep and lands as William's vassals. They were both more than a little pleased at the prospect and eagerly agreed to everything I suggested might be required. They certainly should like the idea; there was nothing we wanted from this place that the Leslies couldn't honourably or otherwise provide.

They were absolutely enthusiastic. Having the honour of Hathersage and its four manors with revenues sufficient to support a knight was obviously beyond their wildest dreams; I think they would have agreed to almost anything.

William and I certainly know the feeling. We'd be wanting it for ourselves if we didn't have Cornwall and know about the coins and opportunities in the Mediterranean ports and thereabouts.

Whilst the two Leslies sat and watched with growing excitement, I took a blank parchment out of the messenger's pouch, sharpened up a goose feather with my one of my wrist daggers, and wrote up our contract. It was a very detailed agreement so it took up almost an entire page. *And, of course, both father and son were very impressed because I know how to read and scribe as all clerics claim and some actually do.*

When I finished scribing on the parchment I read it to them. They liked it right well and instantly agreed. Then, whilst the two Leslies were running around in the rain to arrange the necessary ceremony, I sat under the wagon to stay dry and wrote another parchment—this one to King Richard explaining the situation. Whilst I wrote, the stray dog I'd fed some bad cheese earlier this morning came over to get out of the rain and laid its head on my ankle.

My message to the King was quite simple.

"The Will of God relating to the Earldom of Cornwall and Hathersage Castle and its manors has been determined in mortal combat, as His Illustrious Majesty so wisely decreed. And God has spoken—Cornell is dead of an honourable wound and the King's most loyal and devoted vassal, William of Cornwall, now holds the earldom and Hathersage as his freeholds."

I added, of course, the customary words about William and his heirs and vassals being deeply and eternally grateful to the King for his wisdom and swearing they will always loyally serve him—the usual meaningless blather that means so much to those who are full of themselves and little else. I'll either drop the parchment off at Windsor on my way back to London or, better yet, send it to the King by messenger from London via his chancellor so neither he nor his courtiers have a chance to question me about Cornwall and the archers.

Either way, I'll offer Longchamp some coins

"for his expenses" if he can get the King to sign the parchment decree I enclosed with my message. It grants Hathersage and its lands to William as a freehold. Hopefully, Richard will put his mark and seal on the decree since "God obviously wills it."

******

The commendation ceremony for a feoffment is a very formal affair in front of witnesses, as indeed it should be given its significance. Leslie assembled his men and their families as soon as the rain stopped about an hour later.

When everyone was assembled, Leslie and his son and I stood on a wagon and his men and their families gathered around in the mud and listened intently as Leslie loudly announced his homage and swore his oath of fealty for himself and his heirs and the men of his company.

He and they are now, Leslie announced quite proudly to his men and their families, vassals of William, the Earl of Cornwall, and will be vassals of William's heirs and their heirs after them forever.

Immediately thereafter, as required by custom, I proclaimed, on behalf of William, Earl of Cornwall, that Captain Robert Leslie and his heirs are granted the honour of holding Hathersage Castle and all its lands and manors so long as they meet their obligations to William and his heirs and to the King. *The heir and next in line after William being, of course, his son and my nephew and student, young George.*

It was a stirring spectacle and it began as soon as the rain stopped coming down. Leslie, his son and heir standing at his side, called on his people to bear witness that he was accepting the Earl of Cornwall's offer of the honour of the fief of Hathersage and the stewardship of all its demesne lands and manors. He did so, Leslie announced, under the following conditions which I read aloud from atop the wagon where the three of us were standing.

I read the conditions out quite loudly so Leslie's people standing around the wagon could both see us and hear us — and I read them from the parchment I'd written on, the one on which all the people present would see Leslie and his son and heir make their marks immediately upon it being read out to them.

After reading aloud each specific condition, I turned to the Leslies to get their loud "ayes" and an emphatic nod of their heads, after each of which the assembled people gave a great cheer of agreement. *Can we really do this and it will mean something? I don't know. But it certainly sounds good.*

"Robert Leslie and his heirs agree to pay without delay all of the taxes and charges the King levys on the fief of Hathersage and without delay answer the Earl of Cornwall's levy for some or all of his men of military age."

"Aye." There were great cheers from the people gathered around the wagon—heartfelt and helped by young Leslie waving the palms of his open hands upward to encourage them.

"Robert Leslie and his heirs agree to deliver to the Earl of Cornwall at Restormel Castle three young brood mares in the month of July each year and, in addition, deliver either three journeymen archers possessing their own admirable longbows or six able-bodied young men with strong arms capable of being apprentice longbow archers."

"Aye." More great cheers.

If some of the apprentices are young enough and lively enough, they'll become my students and learn their sums and letters; there's no need to explain such things to the Leslies today but I certainly will in the future. I'm thinking they'll be sending us some lively boys instead of only strong young men.

"Robert Leslie and his heirs agree that each year they will require all men living on their honour of Hathersage to possess and be learnt how to use a longbow and to each month hold an archery tournament on the commons open to all men with a prize of at least three copper coins for the best longbow archer and penalties for those of his men who do not participate."

"Aye." More great cheers.

Leslie's men obviously like the idea of a monthly tournament with prizes; it gives them an opportunity to win extra coins. What they apparently don't yet realise is that now they'll all have to make longbows for themselves. Yew wood is best but properly selected elm will do.

"Robert Leslie and his heirs agree to continue and respect the rights and offices of all churls, franklins, merchants, and gentry on the lands they hold for the Earl of Cornwall, to immediately free all slaves and serfs to be churls or better, and to exact no retribution or the loss of office or home on any person for their losses suffered in the taking of Hathersage and its lands."

"Aye." More great cheers.

"Robert Leslie and his heirs agree to provide the widows and children of Lord Cornell and their own dead and injured retainers with appropriate dower housing and food if they pledge their liege to the Leslies."

"Aye." More great cheers. *Of course, Leslie's people liked this condition; it's everyone's fear they'll be injured or widowed and be left to die of starvation and cold.*

"Robert Leslie and his heirs agree all orders, requests, appointments, and suggestions of the Church and its priests shall be received through the Earl of Cornwall to insure they conform to the wishes of both the Pope and the Earl."

"Aye." More great cheers. *Good. I'm glad William thought of it. There will be no burnings and tortures for the Church except in the very unlikely event William agrees to them.*

And, of course, there are various additional conditions to which Leslie and his son have also agreed that I did not announce. Chief among them: If Lord Baldwin's widow Isabel is discovered she is to be immediately hung or cut down as a murderess most foul; if Cornell leaves a wife or children, they are to be immediately set free and given the honour of one of Hathersage's manors if they will pledge their liege to the Leslies. Another requires the Leslies to immediately start their people building permanent new hovels and return the existing hovels to their owners in good condition with all their personal goods intact.

Actually, there is not enough housing in the village and some of Leslie's people have already started building hovels for themselves; this morning I saw some of the women weaving the wattle that will be daubed with mud and sheep shite to form the walls of their new hovels — to keep the cold and rain out and heat and smoke of their fires in.

Chapter Two

Thomas prepares to return to Cornwall

After the feoffment ceremony, there was as great a feast as the Leslies could organise with the roasting of sheep and much drinking and merriment and games of dice and Moors dancing. *I'm sure the watchers in the castle were perplexed and worried when they saw it from the ramparts. Well, of course, they are; wouldn't you be concerned if your enemies begin rejoicing?*

The next morning Leslie's men pulled back from their positions around the castle — and I put on my bishop's robes and mitre and walked towards the castle drawbridge with a cross in one hand and my crozier in the other. One of Leslie's men walked ahead of me blowing loud noises from some sort of horn and another man walked next to him waving a strip of dirty linen tied to a stick.

Leslie's men pulled up and stopped just out of crossbow range; I kept walking with my cross held high until I reached the raised drawbridge. The men on the battlements of the castle and its gatehouse obviously saw me; they were pointing and more and more faces were appearing at the archer slits to see what the commotion was all about.

I was wearing chain mail under my robes but I had no illusions about my chain stopping an iron crossbow quarrel; all I can do if they loose at me is hope they miss and run like the devil is on my heels. Zigging and zagging back and forth is best.

After some minutes of standing at the edge of the moat the small side door in the great castle gate opened and a very elderly knight clanked out in partial armour, probably all he could wear and still walk. The castle battlements were absolutely full of quiet watchers. No one said a word.

"Who are you, Priest, and what do you want?"

"I am Thomas, Bishop of the diocese of Cornwall, and I bring news of Lord Cornell and the Will of God and King Richard."

******

I'm leaving Derbyshire with Roger and most

of my men. Hathersage's drawbridges are still up and its battlements manned, but a truce is in effect; food is being allowed into the castle, the people in the castle have been informed of the terms under which Robert Leslie will replace Lord Cornell if he is dead, and three horsemen have been allowed to ride out of the castle unmolested to ascertain Cornell's fate.

The terms of the truce are well understood by everyone — there will be no more fighting if the horsemen return and report Cornell is indeed dead; the siege and resistance will continue if they return and report he is not.

Most of my men and I immediately left for London in horse-drawn wains with two of the men on horses as outriders. Only Joseph and four of our archers stayed behind. Two of them will carry the word in horseback to Cornwall when Leslie takes possession of the castle in William's name; Joseph and the other two will ride for London and bring the same word on our next available galley or cog.

There was no sense of anxious hurry as we moved down the rough cart path to the old Roman road that runs towards London. Word had obviously spread about the siege and possible fighting; the path was not as heavily travelled as it might have been. The result was convenient — we had the cart path to ourselves most of the time until we reached the main north-south road between London and the north.

At night the men cooked bread and burnt strips of meat on their camp fires, and slept in the wains and under them. Roger and I shared a sheepskin tent. Sleeping in the wains and our own tent is nicer and safer. The sleeping rooms at the village inns and taverns we reach every six or seven miles are inevitably dirty and dangerous. Moreover, you never know who'll be sharing your room and your bed.

On the other hand, the local ale along the way was uncommonly good and travelling was thirsty work, and there was always sheep shite in the water by the road to make it taste poorly — so we inevitably stopped at each village's inn or alehouse we reached and everyone crowded in to sample its ale. *At each, I gave Roger a few small coins for the alewife so our men could sample the local ale; they did well and they deserve it.*

We had a rather uneventful trip for the first few days even though the spring weather was most foul and sometimes quite chilling even though it is still summer. It rained periodically, and it seemed as if one or another of our wains was continually breaking a wheel or getting stuck in the mud. On the other hand, we didn't meet many travellers coming the other way to block our progress.

Word was out about the siege and possibility of fighting around Cornell's keep—that's for certain because it's always the first thing we're asked about by the people we meet in the taverns and on the road. As you might imagine, we slept safely and soundly; forty or so heavily armed men were not about to be troubled by the outlaw bands, minor barons, and toll collectors who infest the roads—and are often one and the same.

We didn't meet many travellers until we reached the main road between Chester and London. It was the old Roman road running north and south across England so it was a much more improved track to travel on. Even so, we didn't make better time because the number of people and wagons on the narrow road increased in both directions. What particularly slowed us down was frequently getting stuck behind slow-moving travellers with no place for our wains to pass or having to pull over to let fast-moving gentry pass us.

The heavy traffic on the old Roman road slowed us down so much I took to riding next to the hostler on the first wain wearing my mitre and waving my crozier at people to move them aside whenever possible. Mostly they did.

It took us almost a week to reach London.

****** *Thomas*

London was its usual wet and foul self, and the sky was growing dark by the time our wagons reached the stable near the quay. Freddy the stable master was not in the stable, but his hostlers informed me one of our galleys was anchored just off the quay with a couple of our recruiting sergeants and a dozen or so of the archers and apprentice archers they'd brought in.

I immediately handed one of the hostlers a couple of copper pennies and told him to use one of them to hire a harbour boatman to row out to our galley and ask its captain to please meet me in the White Horse tavern at the north end of the quay. The White Horse is where I'm planning to take my men for a drink to help us recover from our long but not uncomfortable trip from Derbyshire.

We were in the White Horse about an hour later when the door opened and in came one of our galley captains. He spotted us through the fireplace smoke and walked over with a smile on his face. It was one of the many Henrys in our company. This one was Henry, the one-time forester from Norwich and one of our very strongest and experienced archers. He'd been rowed ashore by the boatman who carried my message.

His galley, Henry Forester reported, was being rowed up to the quay as we speak and would be moored there and available for boarding within the hour. We can board whenever we want.

"But no need to hurry. We can't leave until the sun begins to pass overhead tomorrow and the morning fog lifts."

Henry was more than a little pleased to pull up a wooden stool and join us for a bowl of the new juniper-flavoured drink we were enjoying and hear the latest news.

This was Henry's first time in London and his first visit to the White Horse. He only arrived a few days ago with our messenger and has been doing his drinking with his pilot at an alehouse at the other end of the quay.

Henry Forester may not be as sharp a lad as Henry from Colchester who is in charge of all of our archers and their training, but he's a damn fine archer and galley captain.

Henry roared with laughter at my tale of the Belgian mercenaries and lamented at not being with us when he heard how we'd gulled them. This was the second time he's missed out on all the fun, he said — not having been there to participate in gulling the mercenaries at Sarum and not being at the mouth of the Tamar during William's skirmish at the river ford when Cornell was killed.

"Ah . . . yes, thank you," Henry told the tavern keeper who comes over with an expectant look on his face when he saw Henry put down his empty bowl with a great sigh of pleasure.

"I wouldn't mind having another bowl of your fine brew. How do you brew it, pray tell? I can't say that I've ever smelled or tasted anything like it before."

Our host smiled and said something about his wife's secret recipe for juniper berries as he picked up Henry's bowl and a couple of others and took them off to be refilled. Then we settled down in the fireplace smoke to tell more stories.

Before the interruption, I'd just started telling everyone about the first time Peter and I brought some of our archer sergeants and men here so they could get horses and ride out to the shires and recruit more archers. *According to Peter, more of them get on backwards or fall off every time I tell it.*

"Henry, did you ever hear about what happened when some of our archers got on horses for the first time? At the stables right around the corner, it was."

Chapter Three

Thomas returns to Cornwall

It was late when we finally staggered out of the White Horse in the dark and climbed aboard Henry's galley to sleep. Most of my men from Hathersage were already on board.

Men were sleeping everywhere on the rowing benches and in between the stacks of supplies and provisions. Henry and Roger and I had pissed against the wall of one of the buildings next to the quay before we climbed over the galley railing so we went straight to the little captain's castle to sleep.

It's been a fine day and I'm just like the rest of my men – seriously drunk and ready for a good night's sleep.

****** *Thomas*

I woke up in the dark early the next morning with a splitting headache from too much of the juniper berry drink. It was early but it was also time to send my parchment message and it accompany decree draft to the King. I'd thought about it quite a bit whilst bouncing along on my way to London and had decided to send the news of Cornell's death the decree for the King to sign via his chamberlain, William Longchamp, the Bishop of Ely — so he'll be able to pocket the coins it implies he'll receive if the King makes his mark on God's decision. I'm hopeful the coins will sweeten Longchamp towards us, let him know we can work together so to speak.

We need to sweeten Longchamp because the good Bishop was the man who sold the earldom to FitzCount to raise money for Richard's ransom and might still be unhappy because we killed FitzCount; he also may have been involved and pocketed some coins when Richard then granted Launceston and the earldom to Cornell. Enough is enough. We've either got to kill the man or buy him.

Longchamp is well known to be among the greediest men in the kingdom. Accordingly, so I reckoned, it would probably save us coins in the long run to buy the Bishop's goodwill when we need it instead of having to continually kill those who get to him and the King before we do. Who knows, there may already be another fool or a highborn second or third son who wants to live in Cornwall or, more likely, prance around the court as an earl. I doubt it but you never know, do you?

In the early morning before the sun arrived, I shook Roger awake and after a piss and some bread and cheese we walked to the livery stable in the lane of blacksmiths behind the north end of the quay. *Oh my poor head; I've got to find out what is put in that drink to make it so powerful; if it doesn't take up too much space, we could buy some and sell it in the ports we visit.*

The sun was just coming up as Roger and I walked in the waning darkness to the stable where we returned our horses yesterday. We were going to the stable early because I need to hire a couple of hostlers to carry my parchment to Windsor. I also want to settle my account with the stable master before we sail. Freddy with the bashed in face is the stable master; his goodwill is important to us because, among other things, Freddy's stable is where our recruiting sergeants tell our newly recruited archers and apprentice archers to come to be gathered up and carried to Cornwall.

It was early and the sun had not yet begun passing overhead, but the stable was already full of hostlers preparing the stable's horses for another day of pulling carts and wagons on the quays and wharves and streets throughout the city. From dealing with Freddy in the past, I knew this is the time we were most likely to find him here without having to search the local taverns and alehouses — and we did.

"Hoy, Freddy. It's good to see you again. I'm sorry I missed you yesterday when we brought the horses and wagons back. How much do I owe you for the two horses we dropped off along the way and the broken wheels?"

"Oh, Eminenz. I seez the horsez and knows you izz back, don't Izz? Izz six silvers each same as last time, izzn't it?"

"All right, Freddy. Six I'll pay — but only if you'll have two of your most dependable hostlers ride out to Windsor this morning with a parchment pouch for the King's chamberlain. His name is Longchamp and he's the Bishop of Ely. They're to hand this message pouch to the guard at the castle gate if Longchamp is in the castle and then return here immediately without stopping along the way; they're to ask where the Bishop is and bring the pouch straight back here if he is not at Windsor.

"No, Freddy, one man won't do; I want two to carry it in case one of the horses breaks down."

I don't want to go in person and risk being questioned about Cornwall and Hathersage or asked for more coins. Delivering my message this way would, I hoped, make it harder for the King to say no to the whole idea or try to make changes in our arrangements with Leslie.

"Oh, and Freddy, if the Bishop is not at Windsor, your men are to ask where he is — but they are to immediately bring the information about his whereabouts and the pouch straight back here to me. They are not to go anywhere else to deliver it or go off to do another task."

It's an important parchment and I need to know it has been delivered before we sail. That's why I'm going to wait on Henry's galley until the hostler returns. I'll have to stay in London to make other arrangements if Freddy's hostler can't deliver it.

******

Freddy's hostlers left immediately and returned as the sun was finishing its move around the world to shine God's light on His sinners. Roger and Henry and I were just starting to tuck into some chops and cheese in the White Horse when in walked Freddy with a big smile.

"Joe and the boy just got back, Your Eminenz. The Bishop waz at Windzor and theyz leaved the pouch at the gate for him just az you zaid."

"That's good, Freddy, very good, it is. Why don't you pull up a stool and join us? Mistress Ann just finished brewing a new batch of her juniper and it's uncommonly good."

We finished our chops, made our farewells, and left as Freddy was once again waving at the barmaid to order another mug of juniper drink. I could see that Henry and Roger want to stay longer, but I was having none of it. *I've sailed before after a night of heavy drinking and it's not pleasant at all.*

I'd leave them here to their folly but I wasn't about to walk back to the galley by myself in the dark. There are too many cutpurses about.

"You two can return to close the place with Freddy if you want, and if you'll promise you'll carry your swords unsheathed and mind the cutpurses. But please remember we'll be in the channel tomorrow on a galley—and the channel's no place to be with a head gone hurtful from Mistress Ann's brew, is it?"

******

The winds and conditions in the channel were not the best. But between hard rowing when it was needed, and Henry's sailor sergeant constantly aiming the sail as only an experienced sailor man knows how, we were able to claw our way south to the mouth of the Fowey in less than a week.

It was a miserable week because my archers and I and the dozen or so new recruits we're carrying were almost constantly seasick even with constant rowing to distract us.

Yes, I sat with the men on the rowing benches and helped them row. They didn't need my help, of course, but I found it better to be active on voyages rather than just sitting idle whilst the galley bounces this way and that. At least rowing gets me tired enough to be able to sleep when my turn at the oars is up.

Even so, my legs felt strange and weak all the way to Cornwall. They didn't feel better until we reached the mouth of the Fowey and began rowing upstream towards Restormel. *It's very strange, isn't it, seasickness, I mean? Too much shaking of the juices is what they say.*

******

A smiling Harold was waiting on our little floating wharf with Andrew Brewer when we bounced up against it and began mooring Henry Forester's galley. Off in the big field beyond the camp, I could see men walking up and down together and others practising their archery and the use of swords and our long-handled bladed pikes. Everything seemed quite normal. It was as if I hadn't been away at all.

"Hoy, Harold, it's good to see you. Are things alright?"

"Oh, aye, Thomas, alright is how things are; indeed, they are. Killed that right bastard Cornell, the archers did, didn't they? Now we can get out of here and head east for some coins."

I had a spring in my step and was brimming with enthusiasm as I started walking up the track towards the castle. The weather was glorious for a change, and behind me I could see our new archers and apprentice archers coming off Henry's galley and looking about anxiously and curiously. They know their lives are about to change—they just don't know how; they're excited about it and concerned. I knew how they felt; I could hardly wait to see my boys and begin putting more learning on them.

Monk's note from a later French parchment: "The English longbow men launch their arrows differently from our archers and the Genoese. Our archers hold their bow stave out in front of them, notch an arrow in bowstring, pull the bowstring back, and then let go of the string to shoot. The English do it differently. They notch an arrow on the string, hold the string and the notched arrow to their ear, and thrust the bow stave out in one big movement as they shoot. The outward push of the bow at the time of launch apparently throws the arrow an even greater distance and yields more accuracy. Our men cannot do it as it requires longer and stronger bows than we have, much practise to learn, and the very strong arms people seem to have in Britain where the weather is always foul."

Chapter Four

Thomas returns and William prepares to leave.

I'm home. Restormel's gate was open and its drawbridge was down. Everything felt normal and relaxed, almost as if I'd never been away. And here comes George and the boys running out to greet me with William and Henry and Angelo Priestly right behind them. *I'm home safe again; thank you Jesus and all the saints.*

"Hello, George; hello, boys," I shouted with great enthusiasm as they came bounding up all full of excitement as only small boys can be. Then it was big hugs for the boys and William and handshakes and back patting all around for the men.

"Is Leslie in the castle?" was William's first question even before I finished my hellos.

"Aye, and happy he is to be there. Ready to settle down, wasn't he?"

"Well," said William as he took my arm, "that's good news, very good news. Now come in and tell us all about it. The boys would like to hear as well, wouldn't you, boys?"

They cheered for me; the boys cheered. I do so love it here.

****** *William*

There was much to discuss when my brother Thomas came home from Derbyshire, particularly when he told me he didn't think we needed to keep any additional men at Hathersage to fight for it—"and, of course, we can always send them them back if trouble arrives."

That was exactly what I wanted to hear. I immediately announced our galleys and archers would sail for Cyprus and the Holy Land ports as soon as we could provision them. *We're leaving late as it is; we should have sailed several weeks ago.*

I'll be going back to Cyprus and the Holy Land with fifteen galleys, one cog, their sailors, and just over fifteen hundred archers—longbow men trained to fight on ships as well as marching about and fighting together on land. That means I'm leaving seven galleys and one cog here—if you include the two galleys being repaired by the boat wrights and the one being torn up for firewood because it was in such bad shape from the wood worms.

Eight of our company's original archers are sailing with me as senior sergeants. As for the other original archers, my priestly brother is staying in command here with Roger as his number two and Martin as the senior sergeant in charge of Launceston.

Three of our other survivors of the original company are still in the Holy Land—Randolph in Constantinople, Bob Farmer in Antioch, and Samuel Farmer on Cyprus where he's in charge of the archers we've already got out there. We fourteen are all that's left of the one hundred and ninety-two of us who went out east crusading with King Richard those many years ago.

We'll also be taking almost four hundred experienced sailors including almost a hundred newly recruited veteran sailors who seem to be qualified to sergeant a cog or be its pilot. *What we've learnt is that any sailor man who can command or pilot a cog can also command or pilot a galley, what with it having a smaller sail and the ability to row its way out of trouble.*

Unlike last fall when we sent our apprentice

archers out to Cyprus for their training, and kept our veterans to fight Cornell, this time we'll do it the other way around. This time we'll only be taking archers out to the Holy Land who are already fully qualified both to fight on land and on the sea, the men we've taken to calling our marines to distinguish them from the archers who haven't yet been learnt how to board ships and fight at sea.

Ever since we returned to Cornwall last year, our newly recruited archers and apprentices have been spending their time learning how to fight under the watchful eyes of Henry and his experienced archer sergeants; similarly, our newly recruited sailors have been learning how to sail the galleys the archers will live and fight on under the command of Harold and his experienced sergeant captains.

We'll also be carrying out to Cyprus some of the English slaves we freed and brought back to England so they could return to their villages and families—and came back to us because they found nothing when they got home. Finally, and last and least, we'll be taking almost all of the foreign galley slaves we carried here on the prizes we took out of Algiers and Cadiz. They've volunteered to help row because they want to return to the Mediterranean where it's warmer, probably so they can get off our galleys along the way and run for their homes.

One of our cogs and our least seaworthy galley will remain here permanently so they can be used for the schooling of our apprentice archers and our new sailors. In addition to learning to use their longbows and bladed pikes, the apprentices need to learn about fighting at sea, climbing grappling lines to board potential prizes, and such like that.

The archer apprentices are particularly keen to be learnt because they won't receive much more than their food and clothing until they qualify as longbow archers and learn how to fight both on land and on board ships. Until they fully qualify as archers and are learnt to fight on galleys and cogs, they'll carry their bows and our new bladed pikes and only fight on land here in England.

It's little wonder that some of the apprentices who have been with us for a while are clearly disappointed they have not been found sufficiently capable as archers to be allowed to go out to Cyprus as marines; they'll neither earn coins for serving nor have any chance of prize money until they do.

****** *William*
Whilst we're gone our other four cogs and their crews will be used to carry messengers and to

make periodic voyages along the coast to pick up new recruits and supplies.

In all, remaining behind under Thomas's command will be almost five hundred archer apprentices who are still not yet strong or accurate enough to push a longbow out for repeated good shots, the sailors for the ships that will be based here, two hundred or so able-bodied men working as shipwrights and smiths and such, and a company of about one hundred and twenty experienced archers to train and sergeant the apprentices and help guard Bossiney, Restormel, and Launceston.

Most, but certainly not all, of the experienced archers who will be staying behind are volunteers who for some reason or another didn't fancy spending months at sea and fighting as marines. Many have women and children they don't want to leave, and a few are either cowards or reasonable men who don't like the odds of fighting in the east and the hot weather.

Until today there had been no announcement of a sailing date or who would be on our ships. That's because I needed to talk to Thomas to find out if we would need to send some of our men to fight for Hathersage Castle instead of sending them to the Holy Land.

Even so, ever since Cornell died everyone has

been expecting an announcement. As a result, over the past few weeks, starting as soon as it became known that Cornell was dead, there have been fevered efforts by the men who fear being left behind to exchange positions with men assigned to the Holy Land galleys who don't want to go.

At first Henry and Harold and I tried to accommodate everyone who wanted to trade positions. But so many applied for a chance to plead to change their assignments, I finally announced that anyone who wished to join the voyage could trade places with someone who did not; and anyone who did not want to go on this voyage could find a qualified substitute and exchange with him.

The possibility they might get killed or drowned or die of the eastern poxes didn't seem to matter much to the most of the archers. Those who were anxious to sail with me to Cyprus and the Holy Land wanted the chance of prize money and advancement no matter how dangerous it might be.

They're right to want to make their marks to go with us; it's right rare when someone not in the gentry has an opportunity to advance himself in England these days. Thomas and I certainly understand about that.

Chapter Five

William sails for the Holy Land.

After we killed Cornell, Harold and Henry and I
and the rest of our senior sergeants spent our days
training the men and getting things ready for our
return to Cyprus and the Holy Land. Peter Sergeant
was usually with us. Peter's now a master sergeant
like Henry and Harold and Yoram in Cyprus. He
lives in the castle as my deputy, my chosen man.

Whenever possible my senior sergeants and I
hold our serious discussions and do our planning
around the long table during our evening supper in
the castle's great hall. We do it at the long table
both for the privacy it gives us and so George and
the boys can listen and ask questions.

Surprisingly, the boys often ask questions,

and good ones at that. They're lively lads and that's for sure.

Thomas says it's important George and the boys understand what we are doing and why. I'm increasingly coming around to his way of thinking.

Helen and Angelo Priestly, the boys' teacher, typically sit with us until the boys begin to yawn and ask permission to go to bed. But they rarely contribute a word—although, sometimes when we're alone, Helen will ask me privately about some of things my sergeants and I have talked about at the table.

Also, I suppose, the women who do the cooking and serving might hear bits and pieces of our plans and thoughts even though I always make it a point never to say anything of significance when they are within hearing distance. *They can't help themselves; women are all gossips and tattletales, aren't they?*

It isn't just our planning for our voyage to the Holy Land we discussed every evening. We also discussed everything from promotions and the training of our archers and prize crews to the question of where we need to build or improve bridges and roads—and where we don't want them built or improved because we want Cornwall to remain isolated from London and forgotten by the

King and his courtiers.

Being forgotten and ignored is important to us. We want to be left alone by the rest of England and particularly by the King and church.

Perhaps it's wishful thinking and my imagination but I think the boys somehow understand why we're talking and consulting our parchment maps in front of them as part of their educations — so they'll know what to do and worry about when they grow up; at least, I hope so.

****** *William*

Thomas's return and the good news about the Leslies changed everything — and the pace of our activity and planning picked up rapidly when I announced we would be sailing for Cyprus and the Holy Land in three days.

Important among the many things to be done now that we have a firm sailing date, is making sure Martin Archer at Launceston knows when we will be leaving and has enough supplies to withstand a siege in case one occurs whilst we're gone.

Our plan is for Peter and I to return late in the autumn; but what if we don't return until the spring or even later? Accordingly, one of the very first things I did the morning after Thomas returned was send Peter to Launceston to inform Martin that we would be leaving in three days — and to make another inspection of Launceston's readiness both for long sieges and surprise attacks.

Then I spent the rest of the morning bringing Thomas up to date on the everyday life of Cornwall and what he'll have to cope with whilst I'm gone. There has been a constantly increasing stream of requests for everyday decisions, particularly from the Cornish-speaking folk who constitute the majority of Cornwall's people.

It seems that the villeins and churls in the Cornish tithes and hundreds are greatly encouraged by my order freeing Cornwall's slaves and serfs to become free churls. Even the people who were already churls and franklins seem pleased.

Unfortunately, and at the same time, my order freeing the slaves and serfs distressed some of the priests and the two abbots and the surviving holders of several of the Launceston manors. *At least, that's what the priests and others have been telling Peter and me when we visited their parishes. But were they telling the truth and what does it mean?*

"Thomas, whilst you've been gone, I've been getting mixed messages about my freeing of the slaves and serfs. On one hand, the villeins and free men seem genuinely pleased; on the other, several of your six parish priests have come and petitioned me, as the archdeacon of your diocese, to reverse the order.

"One particularly nasty fellow, the priest at Saint Ives, is quite angry about losing the serfs who had been working for him on the Church's three farms. The abbot of Bodmin came to see me as well. He's also upset about the monastery losing its slaves and serfs. All I could do was tell them you would soon return and that they would have to be patient until you get back and can instruct them further as to the wishes of the Church."

"Oh thank you, very much," my priestly brother said sarcastically with a wry smile. "And what do you think I should tell such fine churchmen? That you regret the decision and intend to change it since God wants his people to be serfs and slaves?"

"No, damn you, of course not. You know better than that. What I need you to do is spread a bit of olive oil on the waters — and quietly get rid of any of them who start making trouble or drag their feet.

"You know what to do — order them to leave immediately on a crusade or disappear them permanently. The same for the two knights of Baldwin's who survived."

"Have the two knights been making

trouble?"

"Not at all. Not so much as a peep. They're afraid of losing their heads and their manors, and rightly so. But they're the only two left in Cornwall, so take care of them quickly and permanently if they start making trouble. And, for God's sake, don't replace them if they go.

"The same for anyone who is foolish enough to try to take the place of the those who fell trying to stop us. Disappear them quietly as well. Don't make an example of them, mind you, just permanently disappear them without anyone knowing."

"What do you want me to do with any new priests who show up?"

"Do the same for all the priests who show up in Cornwall looking for parishes; question them first as to why they've come and who sent them—and then get rid of any you think might communicate with another bishop or abbot or grand master. Put them on the next galley or cog outbound for Cyprus if you don't have to kill them. Later you can send a parchment to whoever encouraged them to come saying they'd gotten religion and gone off to the Holy Land."

Another decision that has to be made is what to do with Helen. I've been putting it off for weeks.

My problem is simple—I want her with me and I want her safe. I finally decided when Thomas returned. I don't want to chance losing her; she stays. *And she was very unhappy when I informed her of my decision last night.*

"Yes, Master, I understand." *Master? I haven't heard that for a long time; she really is unhappy.*

******

Three days later and the galleys and the muddy riverbank next to the galleys were covered with a hectic mass of people and supplies. Bundles of squawking and struggling chickens with their legs tied together, women weeping and children running around excitedly, and cattle and sheep and pigs bawling loudly after the cords in their legs had been cut so they could be kept alive and unable to move on the galleys for as long as possible until they were eaten.

Other sheep and pigs were being killed and butchered on the riverbank so their meat could be stacked on board and eaten before it rots. How long it will take before their meat rots so much that it can't be eaten, even with lots of salt, will depend, of course, on how warm it is on the galley decks when we're out on the ocean.

We're not taking any deer and boar carcasses with

us; we would, of course, but we've been eating them as soon as our hunting parties kill them in order to save the coins that have to be paid for the chickens, sheep, pigs, and cattle.

Only the galleys that will be heading for Cyprus were tied up along the riverbank. All the others, those that will be staying behind, had been temporarily floated down to the mouth of the river.

Each of the galleys was tied to the shore with a line from its bow to a nearby tree. As a result, they were all pointed upstream and pressed hard against the bank by the river current .

And, of course, as more men and supplies are loaded on the galleys, they settled deeper and deeper into the river and sooner or later got stuck on the river bottom. That meant their swearing and cursing crews had to periodically wade into the river's cold waters to push the arse ends of their galleys further out to where the river was deep enough to once again float them.

Every spare inch of every galley's hull was filled with barrels and skins of water and supplies, stacks of firewood, fresh carcasses of sheep, pigs, and oxen, and, most important of all, bales and bales of arrows for our longbows. The galleys were full and crowded. Until some of the supplies are used up, the rowers will have difficulty reaching the rowing benches where they will sit and sleep.

The galley decks were similarly covered with supplies and with large bundles of squawking chickens and squealing and struggling sheep, cattle, and pigs. They were literally being stacked on top of one another so high that the crewmen will have to walk on some of them to reach the shite plank hanging over the end of each galley. There were even stacks of wattle cages stuffed full of hens on every galley—we'll eat their eggs until we burn their cages to cook them.

Overseeing everything, of course, were the galleys' cats on board to cadge food and catch each galley's inevitable rats. They were the true owners of our galleys and cogs and we people are barely tolerated visitors. Some were slinking around and carefully inspecting whatever was brought on board; others found a sunny spot on top of something and were snoozing or washing themselves. When it gets dark, they'll find someone to burrow in with to get warm. They have favourite people and places.

******

It was well into the afternoon when the lines were finally cast off, the rowing drums began to beat, and our vast armada of galleys began to slowly and carefully move down the Fowey to the estuary at the mouth of the river. That's where they'll join the cog that is accompanying us to help carry our extra supplies. It finished loading this morning when the last bale of our newly produced arrows and pikes was hoisted into its hold.

Henry from Lewes, Peter, and I were on Harold's galley, our biggest with two rowing decks and forty-four oars on each side; we were the last to cast off our mooring lines and begin floating down the Fowey to its mouth. Henry was going out as the master sergeant in charge of all our archers; Harold as the master sergeant in charge of all our sailors and boats.

I could barely pick out Thomas and George and the boys out of the huge crowd standing on the muddy riverbank to see us off. The boys kept waving and running along the riverbank and calling out until the river bent and we were out of sight.

It was the middle of April and 1195 years after our Lord's death, and we were bound for Lisbon as our first port of call and rendezvous. I was pleased and excited to be on my way.

And something isn't right with my sergeants and Harold's galley; I can feel it, but I can't figure out what it is.

"Harold, have we forgotten something?"

Chapter Six

William is surprised.

Our men began to get seasick before we even raised the sail and rowed out of the harbour and into the channel. About the only good thing about being in command of everything is that I have my own little castle at the front of the galley and the men are more likely to make way for me when I need to hurry to the deck railing to barf.

Peter and Henry were soon standing next to me at the railing and looking as queasy as I felt. They periodically joined me in glowering at Harold who was standing nearby on the roof of the stern castle with an amused smile on his face and a mug of farewell ale in his hand. He never gets seasick, damn his eyes!

Thank God I'm not down below on one of the

rowing decks. They are already beginning to smell from all the vomit, and we've not even gotten clear of the harbour.

Ours was the first galley out of the harbour. When I was able to raise my head over the deck railing I could see more than a dozen galleys in a straggly line behind us and the cog tacking to the south on its way out into the channel.

Harold had the men rowing very slowly and our sail was providing some help even though the wind was from the north. His plan was for the galleys to stay together for as long as possible, hopefully all the way to our first rendezvous. That's why Harold had us moving slowly—so the galleys behind us would have a chance to catch up and form on us. We'll all hang lanterns on our masts at night for the same reason. The cog will stay with us as long as the winds are favourable and then meet us at our first rendezvous—Lisbon.

Rowing slowly so the rest of our galleys can catch up and travel with us is not necessary—but it's good practise, even if the men don't know it yet, for what we'll be doing two or three weeks from now.

****** *William*

I was more than a little tired and my legs

were weak and shaky when I finally turned away from the railing, with a totally empty stomach, and attempted to walk over the heaving and pitching deck to my little castle at the front of the galley.

I'm certainly not hungry; but perhaps if I rest for a while, I can regain my strength and my legs will stop feeling so weak.

That's when I got the surprise of my life — Helen was in the forecastle and promptly began giving me orders before I even had a chance to straighten up and shut the wooden door behind me.

"Rinse your mouth with this wine; you'll feel better."

"What are you doing here? You're not supposed to be here."

"Of course, I am. You gave the order yourself. I heard you when you did."

"What? What are you talking about?" *I was stunned by her appearance and starting to get angry.*

"I distinctly heard you say wives couldn't go and that anyone who wasn't assigned to go could trade with someone who was. Well, I'm not your wife; I'm your servant and I traded. So please rinse out your mouth and spit in the shite bucket."

"But. . . ." *Oh my God.*

"There. That's better. Now spit it out and lie down so I can rub your back. There was one of those little black things on your back when I looked this morning and I'm going to get it out as well."

****** *William*

Our trip's first leg to Lisbon was long but not all that difficult. But no matter how hard we tried, we increasingly lost touch with our other galleys in rainstorms and in the darkness of night.

Even so, we periodically came across some of our other galleys and travelled together with them until something else happened to once again separate us. Such periodic meetings twice happened when we put in to the mouths of creeks and rivers and came across one of our sister galleys who was also temporarily visiting to take on water.

For me, once I got my sea legs back, it was like a relaxing vacation what with my woman to cater to my every desire—*and induce some new ones as well*. Even so, after almost two weeks at sea, the entrance to Lisbon harbour was directly ahead of us and it was a welcome sight.

Surprisingly, we were among the very last of our galleys to arrive. Even the cog was already here. One of our galleys, the one captained by Stephen from Coventry, has been here for almost a week.

I wonder how Stephen got here so quickly? Did

he not work his way along the French and Spanish coasts and stop for water?

"Harold, how did Stephen get here so quickly?"

I want to know if Stephen took excessive risks. He's either very good or very lucky — or very dangerous to his men and himself. Lucky men are best, of course.

****** *William*

Lisbon was its usual vibrant self and we enjoyed it to the fullest. Helen was excited by the variety of things in the city's great market, and her pleasure at finding them pleased me immensely. We came away from our daily trips to the market with a number of colourful rugs to keep our feet warm in Cornwall and new bedding and pots for our little forecastle on Harold's galley.

Hopefully, the rugs won't rot in the wetness of the galley. That happens you know; I've seen it myself.

In a corner of the clothes section of the market we found an Arab merchant selling caps and tunics of different colours. He claimed the linen was dyed in Damascus using a new and secret process so the colour won't run. I promptly bought several of each colour and a pot — and soaked them and washed them whilst he watched in amusement.

Then he was absolutely stunned when I ask if

he can provide two thousand caps and tunics in solid red or green or blue and what the price would be either for delivery in Cyprus or in Cornwall. *We need our men to wear something distinctive so we can tell friend from foe.*

Our most important activity in Lisbon was not the shopping to replenish our supplies; it was the gathering up of information about the heathen pirates and, particularly, the latest news about the heathen city Palma. Palma's where we are planning to make our next rendezvous—but only if it's still safe for English ships and their crews. Moslems don't always get along with believers in the true church.

Lisbon's merchants all said Palma is safe for us to visit and they would know; so Palma's where we'll gather next—with Cagliari on the Christian island of Sardinia as our next rendezvous port after that and the alternative destination for those who miss Palma or can't land there for one reason or another.

Our sergeants and men know of our plans and the fact that we will be getting to Cyprus and the Holy Land late because of Cornell's attempted invasion. They undoubtedly were discussing our plans openly with the merchants in the markets and the girls and alewives in the taverns.

It doesn't matter who knows of our plans—it's a

very stupid pirate who would attack a war galley loaded with prime fighting men on their way to the Holy Land.

Surprisingly, less than a dozen of our men deserted in Lisbon even though it's a fine walled city with many entertainments. They ran whilst we were replenishing some of our supplies and waiting for our last two galleys to arrive.

The men who ran were mostly slaves and sailors who don't want to stay with us and end up going back to spend another winter in England. Their loss was more than offset by the men who come to the quay and offered to make their marks to join us.

Harold was very pleased with our intake; he signed up several experienced pilots who know the waters where we are headed. One of them was a slave of the Algerians for many years and speaks the Moorish tongue as well as Harold who'd also been a Moorish galley slave. Henry, on the other hand, was not pleased; there wasn't a single archer among all the men who applied to join us.

Whilst we waited for the rest of our ships, the men enjoy short shore leaves and we slaughtered what's left of the livestock we'd been carrying and bought replacements and other supplies. It was a very conventional rendezvous and quite pleasant indeed.

Our two missing galleys finally came in

together, and two hours later, after instructing their sergeant captains to meet us in Palma, we cast off our mooring lines and were on our way to Palma without having to leave anyone behind to gather up the stragglers. And once again, our ships were filled to overflowing with complaining animals and sacks and barrels and amphorae full of water and supplies.

Our last two galleys and the cog would give their men a shore leave tonight to visit Lisbon's brothels and taverns. They'll leave tomorrow and rejoin us in Palma.

Chapter Seven

Palma and beyond.

Our voyage to Palma was quiet and comfortable. The weather and winds were good all the way although the days turned hot and sunny once we passed Gibraltar. Summer had arrived.

Harold wisely relied on our sail and let the rowers sleep during the heat of the day to keep their arms strong. And, of course, our other galleys copied us and went slowly as well.

Visibility was good and the moon provided enough light at night so our galleys were able to travel together as one big armada—and in so doing, of course, we inevitably scared the crews of every ship we came across out of their wits; they'd inevitably scurry to get out of our way as if the devil himself was on their heels. Only if they'd been

Moorish war galleys would we have gone for them. They're easy to take—their rowers are slaves; ours are archers trained to fight at sea.

****** *William*

Palma is on Mallorca Island. It's a beautiful place and under the nominal control of the Moors called "Berburs" or something like that. Fortunately for us, and the reason we've put in here once again for supplies and to reform our fleet, the local Moslems are once again involved in one of their long-running, religious wars.

I don't know what the religious differences are among the Moslems. But they must be significant and similar to those between the followers of the Pope in Rome and the followers of the Patriarch in Constantinople. The merchants all say religion is why Mallorca's Berbur king is a deadly enemy of the Moslem Caliph who rules Tunis and Algiers on the other side of the Mediterranean.

The fighting and bad feelings between the Moslems may be bad for the local people and merchants, but it was always good for us—because it made the local heathens keen to tell us everything they could about their equally heathen enemies on the other side of the sea.

What they told us when we were here previously turned out to be quite accurate and useful. Hopefully, it will be again. Information about your enemies and prey is always useful.

All and all, as we know from our previous visits, Palma is a fairly civilised place with many Christians and Jews living on the island as farmers and merchants. Genoa and Pisa have had commercial establishments here for years. The tavern and the two alehouses next to the little quay aren't too bad either, just smoky when their cooking fires are lit. The tavern, in particular, has wonderful bread and cheese even though the girls smell bad.

We've come back to Palma once again to get information and because we didn't have any problems both when we rendezvoused here last year on our way to England and when some of our galleys stopped here in September on their way back from England to Cyprus. Once again, that seems to be the case, the locals being friendly, I mean.

Indeed, the local Moslems seem pleased that we'd given the Tunisians a poke in the eye a couple of years ago, and Algerians last year. At least, that's the story we've been told by the local merchants the last two times we touched here last year and on this visit as well. *No one mentioned our raid on Cadiz last* fall, especially the local merchants; its ruler recently changed sides as the Moslems often do and is now aligned with Mallorca's.

Palma's Genoan and Pisan merchants were a different pot of eels. They were like the island's Jewish and Moslem merchants—all smiles and happy enough to take our coins in the market place and pay us to carry their cargos and parchments. But, according to several of the Jewish merchants, the Genoans and Pisans were not at all happy to see us in Palma. They knew about our concession and trading post on Cyprus and feared we'd come here next and set ourselves up to be their competitors.

And, of course, they're right because this is a logical place for us on the route between England and the Holy Land. So someday setting up a post here is exactly what Thomas and I will be doing if our plan for George succeeds. Unfortunately, the day for a post here is still a long way off; so we'll once again do as we did before and tell lies about our intentions—and go all out to convince the local Christians and everyone else that we are friendly and just passing through on our way to the Holy Land.

Of course, we're friendly. It isn't good to shite where you are going to walk and we almost certainly will want to stop here again. Palma a key port for us as we come and go between Cornwall and Cyprus. Even so, the local Christians don't trust us any more than the local Moslems do and I don't trust them, and rightly so.

I also don't trust the local Moslem ruler because he's a Moslem. It's well known that they'll change sides in an instant and cut off your head if one of their priests tells them God wants them to do it or if they start listening to one of their many wives and mistresses. They're like our Christian kings and popes, and that's a fact.

If we ever come here permanently, we'll probably have to take over the whole island and replace all the Moslems with Christians, and agreeable ones at that. And we're a long way off from being strong enough to take over the island. Besides, we have other more important bread to bake.

******

My parchment map appeared to be a copy of an old Roman map with Latin comments and instructions. It showed a city on the southern tip of the island it called Sardinia.

Harold said the city's name is Cagliari and it would be easy for the pilots of our galleys to find. Moreover, he told me with a great deal of satisfaction, the men he recruited in Lisbon and Palma were all highly experienced sailors who'd found Cagliari many times before and would know how to find it again. He'd been there himself before the Moors took his cog and sold him for a slave.

It will be easy for our pilots to find Sardinia, he said. All they have to do is keep their galleys sailing easterly and a little northerly from Palma until they see land. It's a big island so they couldn't miss it. Then all they had to do was sail south along the coast until they come to the end of the island – and that's where Cagliari is located.

According to Harold, when the pilots see Sardinia in the distance, they simply tell their sergeant captain to turn his galley to the right and keep going along the coast of the Island until they come to the city of Cagliari. It would, Harold assured me, take our galleys only a week or so depending on the winds and how hard we row.

Getting there sounds simple and it's very encouraging to know every one of our pilots has been there before.

Harold says such an approach to piloting works like a charm – unless the southerly winds blow you far enough south so you never see the island and just keep going. And even then, he assured me, there would no problem; if for some reason a galley missed the entire island, it would continue on eastward without turning back and make a long run all the way to our next rendezvous at Crete or even on to Cyprus.

I hope Harold's right because I can think of other problems—such as reaching the island on a dark night or during a storm and run aground or running into a whole fleet of the pirate galleys infesting these waters.

On the other hand, it would be good fortune if one of our galleys meets one or two of the pirate galleys or a Moslem cog. Prizes are always welcome, and one or two pirate galleys are no match for one of ours for two basic reasons: we have more fighting men because we don't have slave rowers, and our men are better trained and equipped—fifty or sixty thugs waving swords may be more than enough to take a cargo cog but they're goose soup for a galley such as Harold's with over one hundred archers on board with longbows and bladed pikes.

In any event, our plan was for all our galleys to rendezvous in Cagliari even though we've never put in there before. Harold and his pilots assured me it had always been a friendly Christian port and our custom would be welcome.

Chapter Eight
A raid is announced.

Cagliari was beautiful to look at from a distance. We were all on deck looking at the city as our galley slowly rowed into the harbour. Harold headed for the big quay that runs almost all the way around the north end of the crowded harbour. The harbour itself was crowded with shipping, including a number of our galleys. Our cog, however, had not yet arrived.

Dinghies from our galleys in the harbour began being rowed towards us almost immediately, and men began coming off those of our galleys moored at the quay and walking towards the vacant place on the quay where we'd soon be berthed.

Something's up. I could see it in the extra anxiety that somehow seems to be accompanying our dinghies and the men who were walking down the quay to meet us. The quay itself seemed strangely deserted for having so many ships in the harbour.

Twenty minutes later, we were tied to the quay and every one of our sergeant captains in the harbour was on our deck. The situation quickly became more understandable and quite worrisome.

There is great tension in the city and the market is closed. For the past several days, there have been riots and looting.

"It started right after we arrived," Gregory Farmer said with a touch of disgust in his voice.

"The new bishop had the local king or prince burn some people in the city square. Horrible, it was."

"He's right," said another of our sergeant captains. "I was in the market arranging for firewood and saw the whole damn thing. It was the damn Roman priests doing it; yes, it was."

"Roman priests?"

"Aye, William, it was the Roman priests. The priests claimed the man was a heretic, but merchants say the real reason they burned him was because he was the steward of the Orthodox Church's manors in this part of Sardinia and refused to surrender the manors to them."

We stayed on the galley that first evening, and Harold ordered all of our men to stay aboard their ships rather than go ashore. It is wise precaution. Two of our sailors on the first galley arriving here had been knifed and robbed by the mob that had taken over the city and burned and looted its shops.

It's a good thing Thomas is going to disappear any priests who show up in Cornwall without being invited; they're vicious and conniving bastards and always trouble; yes, they are.

****** *William*

Helen and I went ashore the next morning to visit the market which had reopened. I took a large guard of men, and it's a good thing I did. Cagliari may look beautiful at a distance, but up close it was truly horrible and its people unhappy and afraid.

Groups of idle and angry-eyed young men stared at us as we passed, and beggars and destitute people were everywhere. Many people were obviously living on the streets and starving. It reminded me of the poorer sections of Alexandria we had walked through when we went to kill the Tunisians who tried to assassinate me after we took their galleys.

We found the Cagliari market open and the

merchants both subdued and anxious to talk. They confirmed what our galley captain told us — many of the people crowding the city are Orthodox Christians, refugees fleeing from the religious conflict in Sicily.

I wonder if the refugees would pay to be carried to Constantinople; that would certainly put them out of the pot and into the fire, but it's probably where the Orthodox would want to go. Or perhaps they'd want to go elsewhere; but where?

Some of the Jewish merchants in the market were particularly willing to talk. They say the local problems began because of succession problems on the Island of Sicily, several days sailing to the east.

Apparently, the King of Sicily just died and the new king, only four years old, has somehow come under the control of a new archbishop — one appointed by the Pope instead of by the Orthodox Patriarch in Constantinople as everyone had expected. The burning of accused heretics and general repression by the new church authorities from Rome was the result. It was causing many of the Orthodox Sicilians to flee to Sardinia to escape.

****

Sleep did not come to me that night. I stayed awake trying to decide if we should send some of our galleys to Sicily to pick up refugees. Or would one side or the other see it as interfering and put us on the enemies' side of their ledger? It kept me awake. Finally I got up and went quietly out of the castle and stood at the deck railing looking at the stars. Should we send our galleys to earn coins in Sicily or not?

It was an important question because we do business with both the Christians who obey the Pope in Rome and the Orthodox Christians who obey the Patriarch in Constantinople. Thomas says only a fool takes sides in a religious squabble; and he ought to know, being as he's a priest and read nine books when he was in the monastery. *I wish Thomas was here; he'd know what to do.*

In any event, it seems the Pope's priests were beginning to use the same methods of terror and false accusations here to turn Sardinia into one of the Pope-controlled Papal States, as Sicily had just become. The Orthodox believers living here and elsewhere on Sardinia, including the refugees from Sicily, were understandably worried and upset about the arrival of the Roman priests.

As it had been explained to me by one of the merchants earlier in the day, Sardinia has four principalities and each of the four princes is somehow associated with Genoa, whose priests answer to the Patriarch in Constantinople as members of the Eastern Church; or, at least, their priests used to answer to the Patriarch.

The merchants think the newly arrived Roman priests are making false accusations to weaken the gentry who look to Genoa and Constantinople — so they can take over their lands and weaken the authority of the local prince until he agrees to make his principality a Papal State and give more power and revenues to the church.

What was interesting and very clear was that the merchants really don't care who is the prince or what religion dominates the island, so long as they are left alone to earn their coins.

But what was even more interesting is why the local prince, who apparently follows the teachings of the Patriarch, would let the Roman priests do this. There is a lesson to be learnt here, but I'm not sure what it is. I wish Thomas was here to help me make inquiries and decide whether or not it is wise to carry refugees.

"But why would the local prince let the burning happen, let alone conduct it at the request of the Roman priests?"

That's the question I asked the merchants the next morning when the market reopened; every one of them offered a different answer.

What's so strange was not that they didn't know

the answer to my question; it was that they didn't seem to care. Or, perhaps, they were too afraid to share their real thoughts. I need to go back to the market tomorrow and ask more questions.

******

A number of Roman priests were waiting on the quay when Helen and I and my rather substantial number of guards returned from the market. So were a large number of refugees seeking passage and men wanting to make their marks and join our company as fighting men or sailors.

We took a lot of guards with us when we went to the market. This places feels like it's about to burst.

The priests were Templars and their sergeants. I could tell because their robes had Templar crosses and were filthy with years of spilled food and unwashed shite. And they were pushy and arrogant as Templars always are; even worse than the Hospitallers, aren't they? They were waiting on the quay next to the galley so someone on the deck must have told them I was in command and would be back shortly.

It's time to play the role Thomas suggested for us both.

A tall, hawk-faced priest addressed me in Old French—and was surprised when I replied in

Latin; and even more surprised with what I said.

"You there, sailor. Who are you and why are you here with these galleys?"

"Who are you to ask?" I responded rather arrogantly. "And why do you ask since you've already spoken to my men and know who I am? Surely the Pope did not send a Templar with a poor memory to assist me."

"Assist you? What do you mean assist you?"

Good. He's surprised.

I didn't answer. I just stood and looked him over for a long moment. Then I asked the Templar my own question with my head cocked and and a smile on my face.

"Who are you, Templar, and why are you here in Cagliari and on this quay?"

You're here to burn people to get control of their lands, aren't you?

"I am Father Antonio of San Marino, a Templar from Sicily and soon to be Archbishop of Sardinia. These are my brothers."

"Ahh, well, greetings to you, Father Anthony," I responded rather arrogantly with the smallest of an acknowledging nod as I identified myself as the Earl of Cornwall.

'Soon to be the archbishop' means the Templars are just now buying the position; probably, they've sent

in the required coins and have not yet received the official proclamation from Rome.

"I am William, the Earl of Cornwall. I'm stopping here on my way to the Holy Land at the request of Pope Innocent himself—to carry Orthodox refugees away from Sardinia so as to weaken their influence on the local people and increase the revenues they send to His Holiness."

Such ox shite. But he'll never know if it's true, will he?

Mentioning the Holy Father and lying about him sending me here worked the gull I intended. A somewhat subdued Father Anthony and I then nodded our heads to acknowledge each other.

"Please let me know if there is any way I may be of assistance to you," I said pleasantly with the most winning smile I could muster. "I will be sure to mention our encounter and your support to His Holiness when I send my next tithe and report."

"I am pleased to know you are of the true faith, Lord William. Please come to me if my brother Templars and I can be of assistance." And, with that, he nodded and turned away.

"Are you sending coins to the Pope?" Harold asked incredulously as the priests turn and stalk away.

"Of course not, are you daft?"

But why did the Templars come to visit me? To take my measure or to warn me away? It certainly wasn't to introduce themselves and be pleasant – to find out my intentions and take my measure probably.

****** William

Cagliari is a foul and dangerous place. The city's crowded streets were even dirtier and less safe than London's. So it was little wonder people want to leave and large numbers of them were coming down to the quay to see if we would give them employment or carry them away as passengers.

Their anxiety to leave sounds encouraging – carrying refugees is what we do to enrich ourselves. *But why aren't they leaving on fishing boats or the other ships in the harbour? Is it fear of pirates or what?*

"Harold, I would appreciate it if you and Peter would talk to the people who come to the quay seeking positions or passage – see if any of them are willing to pay ten gold bezants or the equivalent for passage to Constantinople or Antioch, or five to Cyprus. We'll leave a galley or two here to carry them if there are enough of them who will pay. They'll have to help row, of course.

"Oh, and Harold, would you and Peter also please ask everyone who wants to leave why they have not gone out on one of the fishing boats or other boats that have called in here recently. Also ask them where else they'd be willing to pay to go.

"And one more thing—tell the sergeants to keep their men on the galleys as much as possible and to stay away from the priests; this place is becoming much too dangerous for shore leaves. Be sure the sergeants explain to their men why they cannot go ashore." *Some will sneak ashore for the drink and women despite the order; I hope we don't lose too many.*

******

Harold and Henry and I and everyone else breathed sighs of relief when our cog entered the harbour two days later. It was the last of our ships to arrive and we'd begun to worry about it. Unfavourable winds had kept it away for days.

We were relieved to see the cog both to know it is safe and because it had a company of ninety experienced archers on board, men we'd need for the next leg of our voyage. It also had something in its cargo hold important for our immediate plans— bales and bales of English-made, longbow arrows with iron tips.

Surprisingly enough, the cog didn't run into any pirates even though it was travelling alone. Lucky for them, the pirates, I mean; the cog was carrying ninety archers and trolling for pirate galleys in addition to carrying its cargo of weapons. *It would have pretended to be a cargo cog until the pirates threw their grapples and boarded it — and then thrown its own grapples whilst our archers poured out from wherever they'd been concealed.*

By the time the cog arrived, I knew that Cagliari and its market were best seen from afar. The place was a tinderbox ready to burst into flames; already two of our men have been killed walking in the dark and filthy alleys near the quarter where most of the taverns and prostitutes are located.

We needed every man for where we'd be going, and we certainly didn't want some kind of religious fighting and chaos to delay our departure. Accordingly, Harold ordered our men not to leave their ships except on business, and Henry stationed some of our steadiest men near the gate in the city wall to stop them from slipping into the city.

And, of course, a few of them ignored the order and left the quay area for one reason or another; they'll be stranded and good luck to them if we leave without them.

****** *William*

Thirteen galleys would be sailing with me when we leave — which would be as soon as the time and weather were right for the next leg of our voyage.

We had fourteen galleys, but one sailed yesterday with a full load of refugees at the oars and a skeleton crew of sailors and archers. It was bound for Constantinople — and Harold's galley was now carrying a new chest of coins.

Most of the departed galley's ninety or so archers were transferred to the other galleys to make room for more refugees. The dozen or so longbow-equipped archers who remained on board should be sufficient to see off any pirates — they are under a very capable sergeant, an archer who has been trained in organising a galley's defence using its desperate passengers and the swords and bladed pikes our galleys always carry for our sailors and passengers to use.

We didn't expect the refugee galley to have trouble. These days the pirates rarely attack war galleys, and particularly English galleys with archers and rowers who can join the fight because they aren't chained slaves.

Indeed, if they aren't facing a large number of pirate ships, the archers on our refugee galleys are more likely to see a couple of pirate galleys as potential prizes and chase after them rather than considering themselves victims and trying to escape.

Phillip's experience was a good example. Last year he was carrying refugees from Acre to Cyprus when he came upon a fleet of a dozen or more pirate galleys. He continued towards them and passed through the entire pirate fleet with his archers raining a steady stream of death on everyone they could reach.

The Moors scattered to get out of his way. Although, to be fair, he had passengers with swords crouched all along the deck railings to cut any grappling lines; if there had only been one Moorish galley, he'd have used his archers to clean its deck and boarded it.

****** *William*

Whilst we waited for the right time and weather to sail, the quay was a beehive of activity. Our men were no longer allowed to go into the city, so the city came to them—stalls for everything from women and strong drinks to cooked foods and clothes sprang up almost instantly all along the quay and the beach area next to it. It began only an hour or so after the word went out that our men would no longer able to enter the city.

Our cog was similarly stripped of it archers. It would remain anchored in the harbour until the two galleys which boarded its archers returned them. The archers coming off the cog brought its entire cargo of arrow bales with them. They'd be distributed to the other galleys after we clear the harbour.

One of the galleys which received the cog's archers and arrow bales joined was Archie's. That's the one the one on which Peter and I will be temporarily sailing. Harold and Henry will each be on their own galleys. Our three galleys would each lead one of our attack groups in the raid we're about to launch.

******

It was just after dawn on a warm Wednesday morning, June 9th. The merchants' stalls along the quay were deserted as they have been ever since our galleys and the cog moved away from the quay yesterday afternoon to spend the night at anchor in the harbour. The sky was clear; it was time to begin.

"Wave the flag to call the captains," I ordered Harold.

Within minutes, dinghies were pushing off from the galleys floating around Harold's galley and rowing over to us. I shook hands and enthusiastically greeted each of the sergeant captains as they came aboard. It didn't take long before the various sergeant captains were leaning against the deck rail or sitting on the deck in front of me with their legs crossed.

They were all obviously excited and trying not to show it. *And so was I, for that matter.* They knew something's up—and they were right.

The sergeant captains cheered and clapped when I announced our destination and the plan—and then again when I announced the prize money for each prize reaching Cyprus and how it will be divided among the sergeant captains, sergeants, and men.

"We're going to Tunis—and then we'll go on to Malta to reorganise and reassign our men depending on the number of prizes we have to send to Cyprus. Most of our galleys and all our prizes will head for Cyprus in one great armada after their crews are reorganised and reassigned at Malta; a few will return here first in order to return the cog's archers to the cog so it can again sail out as a pirate-taker."

Our captains were experienced raiders, every one of them. Every captain listening to the plan had been on at least three of our major cutting out expeditions into a big Islamic port and many on all four.

The last time we went into Tunis it was with

five galleys and two or three hundred partially trained men; this time we'd be going in with fourteen galleys, over a thousand archers, and dozens of prize crews for the galleys and sailing ships we hoped to take as prizes.

"This," I told my avid listeners, "is not going to be just a cutting-out expedition to take a few Moorish galleys as prizes and run off with them as we've done in the past. This time we're going to try to take everything that floats—and even take and loot the city if we can.

And this time, everyone in the fleet will share in the prize money according to his rank—because some of our sailors and archers have been sent away to carry refugees and others will be fighting in defensive positions and not directly involved in the taking of prizes.

It took several hours for Harold, Henry, and I to lay out the details of our plan and answer the inevitable questions. Spirits were high and the sergeant captains enthusiastic by the time they returned to their galleys to inform their men.

From the sound of cheers that periodically came rolling over the water to us from the various galleys, it would seem the sergeants and men liked what they were hearing from their sergeant captains.

******

We rowed out of the harbour and sailed closely together all afternoon and the moonlit night that followed. *So close, there were several collisions causing minor damage and many near misses.*

Late the next morning our tightly grouped armada of galleys reached the isolated inlet we were seeking that was several hours rowing from the entrance to the Tunis harbour. We'd wait here until it was time to launch or raid. While we waited, we organised ourselves into four separate smaller armadas.

Harold and Henry and I shook hands and then I moved to take command of my particular armada when Jeffrey's galley came alongside so Helen and I could climb on board. *Helen came with me; I remember what happened to Richard's women; I'm not leaving her with anyone except Thomas.*

From his galley, Harold and his second, Archie the miller who is a sergeant captain himself, will command one of our three armadas. Their five galleys will try to take as many as possible of the Tunisian ships anchored in the harbour.

Harold is the master sergeant of all our sailors, so poor Archie's been hovering in his shadow ever since we left England. Jeffrey's now in the same situation with me on board.

Three hours later and the wind was difficult but not impossible for taking sailing cogs out of the Tunis Harbour. It was time to do what we'd come to do.

Chapter Nine

We raid the Moors of Tunis.

Everyone took a last piss, wolfed down a piece of cheese and part of a flatbread if they were hungry, and got a mouthful or two of wine squirted from a wine skin one of the archers carried around for everyone to enjoy and moisten their mouths — we then we came through the entrance to the Tunis harbour with the rowing drum of every galley beating a fast and steady beat and two men at every oar.

Three of our galleys under Henry's command were assigned to the Tunisian galleys beached off to the left of the two great Tunis quays; six galleys under my command, and carrying a majority of our archers, were going to the quays and the city gates; and Harold's five galleys with a number of prize crews were going for the shipping anchored in the harbour.

The size of the prize crews was larger for those assigned to cogs and other sailing ships and quite small for those assigned take a galley. That's because all the prize crews for galleys have to do is use their rudders and give orders to the slaves on their rowing benches. Those for the cogs, on the other hand, need to have both archers to fight their way aboard and a number of sailors capable of handling their sails.

Peter and I would each be leading three of the six galleys going to the two great stone quays and then to block the city gates. All six were crammed full to overflowing with a large number our strongest archers as well as several dozen prize crews for the ships and galleys we hoped to find tied up along the Tunis quays.

As soon as Peter's and my galleys reach our assigned places along the quays, our archers will jump off and we'll each lead our galleys' archers at a run to one of the two city gates. Jeffrey will then be, once again, in command of his own galley until I return.

My personal galley's assignment is the northern quay, and my archers and I are going for the northernmost gate facing the harbour; Peter will be at the other quay and leading the archers going for the city gate facing the southern part of the harbour. Whilst we are leading our archers to the city gates, the prize crews and a smaller number of archers from our galleys will be going for prizes from among the ships moored along the quays in front of the city wall.

Helen nodded her head and agreed when I told her, quite sternly as a matter of fact, that she will only be allowed to stay outside on the deck in front of our forecastle and watch until the fighting starts — and then she absolutely must move inside with the door barred during the fighting.

She's a curious little thing, and I know her well enough that I quietly arranged for Jeffrey to assign one of his most dependable sailors to move her inside when the fighting starts and guard the door.

****** *William*

Tunis is a great city with a superb harbour. Its two long, stone quays are close to the city wall and the two gates that serve them. It's an altogether impressive place with a couple of beautiful white sandy beaches. The huge dome of a mosque can be seen rising far above the city walls.

Beyond the city walls to the left, houses with red tile roofs are inside walled compounds. They run all the way up to the great fortress on top of the hill that towers above the walled city and harbour. To the right are great open areas where the desert people camp, the city's caravanserai are located, and the city's huge livestock market operates — where everything from camels and horses to slaves and cattle is constantly being bought and sold.

On the beach, particularly to the left of the city walls, are boatyards with a number of galleys and other boats under construction or repair and many more beached and out of use.

More than fifteen thousand people are said to live inside the city walls and another ten thousand beyond them. And they are all apparently either pirates or merchants or their slaves and servants and overlords.

Also, depending on the time of the year, there are often as many as ten thousand desert people in the caravanserai and camping outside the city along the nearby little river that runs into the sea from somewhere in the interior.

The desert people camping outside the city walls along the river are a source of uncertainty and concern. I know they're there because I can see their tents all over the place and smell them all the way out here on the air drifting out from the shore.

Will they rush to help fight us off or not? It concerns us all because we don't know how many of them are here or how they will fight or what weapons they'll use if they do.

Hopefully, they'll be like the Saracens we

fought for Richard and Lord Edmund—lots of boasting and no armour or bottom. In other words, geese for our archers to pluck. The problem, of course, would be that there are so many of them.

******

It was midday Friday, the Islamic Sabbath, and many people and ships' crews, we hope, are at the mosque. Even so, many people were standing on the beach and on the quay watching as we rowed in. There were a lot of us and we were coming fast, so it's little wonder they were looking.

Perhaps we're too early and the prayers and sermons haven't started yet; well, it's too late now. We're committed.

We were barely a third of the way into the harbour when I saw the first of the watchers begin running for the city gates to escape and sound the alarm; others began running toward the galleys on the beach to confront us.

Unlike our previous prize-taking raids, our fighting men are not evenly distributed with each of our galley captains responsible for cutting out as many prizes as possible.

This time our strategy will be different in several ways—for one, we'll have archer-heavy forces under the command of me and Peter going all the way to the two city gates facing the two long quays.

We'll disembark from the six galleys and, instead of our archers staying on the decks of our galleys and trying to keep the heathens off the quays as we've done in our previous port raids, we'll disembark and try to reach and hold the gates to block them before they can get out of the city to attack our prize crews and rejoin their ships.

Hopefully, this will give our prize crews more time so they can get to all the ships moored along the quay — and everywhere else including those anchored in the harbour and nosed in along the beach.

In other words, instead of staying on our galleys next to the quay and using our archers' longbows to fight off the Moslems trying to get at our prize crews as we've done in the past, this time we'll protect them by keeping the Moslems penned up inside the city walls so they can't attack in the first place. *At least, that's the plan.*

Similarly, whilst Peter and I are leading our archers to the city gates, Henry will be leading three other galleys with a large number of prize crews to get the galleys nosed in side by side all along the beach. He too will disembark a force of archers to move inland a few paces and cover his prize crews with their longbows.

Only Harold's five galleys going after the ships in the harbour will be archer light. They will have some, of course, to fight their way past the sailors on the cargo boats anchored in the harbour but nothing comparable to the numbers we'll have on the beach and at the city gates.

Chapter Ten

Archer Sergeant John Putney's experience

Henry promoted me to sergeant and assigned me to lead the archers on Harry's galley when our prize crews go after the Tunisian galleys beached along the edge of the harbour. As we approached the beach, me and my mates could see that there were a lot of galleys along the shore and on the beach, mostly next to what appears to be a shipyard for the repair and construction of all kinds of galleys and fishing boats.

My archers and I are as prepared and determined as men can be. This is the chance of a lifetime for all of us to become rich and rise above ourselves. As you might imagine, I am determined not to let the opportunity pass and neither, I am sure, are my archers.

No less than seven prize crews are on each of the three galleys going after the galleys on the beach. Every prize crew, so every prize crew's sergeant claims, is ready and anxious to fight their way on to a Tunisian galley and take it off the beach. Then, God willing, they'll sail them on to Malta and Cyprus and we'll all be rich.

It's the job of me and my men to use our longbows to keep the heathens far away from our prize crews whilst they either take or burn all the pirate galleys on the beach and nosed in along it. Only when the prize crews finish their taking and burning will master sergeant Henry wave the signal flag and we'll rush back to our own galleys and row them away to safety. *At least, that's the plan; God willing, it will work.*

As you might imagine, we want our prize crews to cut their prizes out and get away quickly before the heathen bastards even begin to fight back. But it's good luck to the Moors if they want to fight. We'll each be carrying a bale of longs and me and my lads know how to use them.

****** *John Putney*

Harry's our captain and Little Ralph the big fisherman is the sergeant of our sailors. I can see them in the bow from where I'm now sitting on the rowing bench which is my home when we are at sea. At the moment, we're rowing up to the shoreline of the beach and me and most of our archers are still on the rowing benches—but ready to pick up our longbows and jump on to the beach as soon as the order is given.

Ralph and Harry are particularly looking for Tunisian galleys which are merely nosed into the beach just south of the quay and still floating—so one of our prize crews can quickly push it off the beach and climb aboard to kill any Moors we find and start the slaves to rowing it out of the harbour and on to Malta.

If a galley doesn't have slaves to row it to Malta, the prize crew is supposed to push it off into the water and go look for one that does. Later, if we have time, we'll tow out those we find without slave rowers when we leave or burn them if we have enough time.

"Over there. Put us in there," I heard Harry shout to Ralph as he pointed at something. Then came the order we all were expecting. "Archers ship oars. Archers on deck."

As I picked up my bow and three quivers and prepared to lead my archers on to the beach, I heard Little Ralph repeat his order to the rudder man. A second later I was on the deck and could see both Harry and Ralph pointing to a string of galleys nosed into the shore so our rudder man and rowing sergeant would know where to go. I had an arrow notched and so did all my men.

"Stand by to back oars . . . back oars."

There was a grinding noise for a couple of seconds as the bow of our hull begins to come over the sands and pebbles of the beach. The jolt of the hull hitting the shore almost threw me off my feet — and certainly saved the heathen who was running towards the beached galleys from the arrow I was about to launch.

His reprieve was only temporarily — Sweaty Bill put a shaft through him just as I began to push my bow out for another shot. So I adjusted my look and pushed a long into the heathen running behind him. Then I leaped over the front deck railing and into the knee deep water.

"Good luck, John," I heard Little Ralph shout to me over the noise of the archers and prize crew men around me as my men and I vaulted over the side of the galley and began sloshing our way up to the beach.

It was all quite thrilling. Even before we finished coming to a stop, there had been great cheers and shouts and about half the men on the deck, the men of my galley's seven prize crews, began to leap over the rail on either side of me to wade ashore and go for the galleys. Every prize crew sergeant was a volunteer because a promotion to be the sergeant captain of his own ship was on offer if he and his crew were able to get their prize to Cyprus.

The sergeants like me, John from Putney, who didn't get selected to lead prize crews are jealous of those who were selected and rightly so since they'll sew on another stripe and become sergeant captains if they are successful. *Even so, it's a good thing to be an archer sergeant and I ought to know; I'm one and that's why I'm leading the archers of our armada's blocking force on the strand.*

There are ten men in each of our prize crews going for the galleys on the beach — four sailors and six archers. Not at all enough if there is serious resistance. The sailors are carrying ships' shields and either swords or pikes; the two archers, longbows and quivers. One sailor in each prize crew carries a bundle of twigs and a lantern to fire them if his prize crew comes across a galley they cannot take because it has no slaves to row it or it cannot be pushed out into the water to be towed.

"Archers, follow me," I had shouted as I jumped in the water and repeated the call I'd practised so many times on the bank of the River Fowey.

My archers poured up from the rowing benches, paused for a split second to grab up a bundle of arrows in addition to those already in their two quivers, and jumped into the water to follow me.

It was up to my knees and cold, but I hardly noticed it. My bow was strung and I was holding it as high over my head to keep my bowstring dry. *Some of our arrows are going to get wet but that won't matter if we use them before the wood warps.*

****** *Harold*

Removing the weight of John's archers and the men in the prize crews from the front of my galley raised our bow and, as I expected, we floated free.

One of my sailors jumped down into the water with a mooring line as my prize crews and John and his archers vaulted over the railing and sloshed their way toward the beach. The sailor's name was Ben and he was an apprentice miller in Yorkshire before he ran away to be a sailor. I chose him to hold the mooring line because he was one of my steadiest men.

Ben will stand out there near the waterline,

knee-deep in the water, and use the mooring line he's holding to keep our galley close to shore so the archers John has led ashore to be our blocking force can get safely back on board when it's time for us to leave. Three others of my sailor men were on deck holding long-bladed pikes and ready to help push us away from shore for a fast departure, as soon as the last man finally scrambles back on board — and the last man had best be Ben or else I will cut him down myself if Ralph doesn't. *We're not leaving anyone behind.*

Except for Ralph and a couple of four-man sailor teams armed with pikes and swords, which I'm holding to use as reinforcements if one of our prize teams needs help, there was no one left on board other than three sailors with pikes and me and the rudder man. We will be up shite creek for sure if John and his archers don't come back to help row us out of here.

****** *Harold*

So far, so good. John from Putney and his archers were on the beach with nobody in range who needed to be killed. Already some of our prize crews were climbing on to the decks of the galleys floating next to us with their noses up on the beach. Others were dashing down the beach to other galleys.

The sand was loose and deep up on the beach where the sand was dry — so our men were running along the water's edge where the footing was firmer and they could run faster. I could see the prize crews and archers from our other two galleys similarly pouring out on to the beach on either side of us.

A minute or so later and there were shouts and screams and the sounds of fighting coming from one of the nearby galleys. *Uh oh. They need reinforcements and fast.*

"Bobby," I snapped to the sailor sergeant standing next to me holding a pike as I point at the beached galley down the beach where the noise and fighting is coming from, and the Moors seem to be gathering.

"Take your men down the beach and join the prize crew fighting for that galley, the third one down; Charlie, you take your men and help clear the two galleys next to us. Come back or engage elsewhere as soon as you finish."

There was shouting and running men but not much fighting all along the beach. But we had a problem, a big problem — it appeared that the prize crew Bobby was off to reinforce had run into a wasp's nest of Saracens and more seem to be heading there. *Damn. Look at all the bastards; Bobby and his lads may not be enough.*

"Everyone, follow me. Emergency. Emergency. Let's go. Hurry, boys, hurry."

I grabbed a pike and a ship's shield off the railing and rushed down the beach at the head of my three pike men and Ralph and Joe the rudder man. We left Ben holding the mooring line without a single man left on board.

Our rushing towards the scene of the fight tipped the balance. Several of the Tunisians saw us coming and jumped off into the water from the galley deck where they'd been fighting our prize party. Others continued to fight but the tide of the battle was definitely turning and the pikes we were carrying were taking a deadly toll—the Moors on the beach began to run and those who stayed on board to fight were quickly cut down.

"Everybody off except the prize crew," I shouted as soon as the last of the Moors fighting on the galley went down. "Everybody off and help push this bastard off the beach. Hurry, lads, hurry."

"Push it out. That's it. Push it out. Is everyone off except Andy's prize crew? Back to our galley. Hurry, boys, hurry.... Run, damn you, Charles, run."

Chapter Eleven

The raid develops.

My lieutenants and I have divided what needs to be done so that each of us to leads a different element of our attack. I've moved over to Jeffrey's galley with Helen and some of the archers I'm going to lead to one of the city gates in front of the city's long quay. A few minutes ago Jeffrey told everyone to piss on the deck, and now the rowing drum is beating at an unsustainable rate. I can feel my heart pounding and I'm glad I pissed when everyone else did.

I don't know why, but it seems a lot of men always need to piss before a battle. I know I always do. It seems strange, but there you are.

Jeffrey has our galley headed for the ships and galleys tied up along the longest of the two stone quays stretching out in front of the city wall running in front of the harbour. Our designated place, among the three galleys heading for our assigned place along the quay, is in the middle of whatever shipping is tied up along it.

One of our galleys is coming even faster, too fast I think, and pulling alongside of us. It is going to unload its archers and send its prize crews after the galleys and cogs moored to the quay to our left.

The other galley in our set of three will unload its archers, and then its prize crews will go after the Moorish ships moored to our right whilst the archers run with me for the city gate.

Jeffrey began to shout his orders as we approached the quay.

"Rowers, stop." And then after a very brief pause, he shouted what the rowers expected to hear next. "Back oars. Pull. Pull. Pull. Pull. Prize crews and deck archers. Get ready. Prize men and deck archers. Get ready."

There was a hard bump and the sound of splintering wood as we banged into the quay in an open space between two cargo cogs. An Arab standing on the deck of one of them was gaping at us in disbelief with his mouth open.

We hit so hard the upper part of our deck railing splintered and was pushed in — so hard some of us who were standing ready to leap on to the quay lost our balance. We quickly recovered and instantly vaulted on to the deck railing and from there on to the quay. Within seconds the archers and prize crews on Jeffrey's galley were pouring off the deck behind me and we were on the quay, and I was running for the gate in the city wall.

For a moment, as I was getting ready to vault over the deck railing, I caught a brief sight of Peter jumping down from the deck of his galley on to the other quay, at least I think it was Peter. Then he was lost from sight and mind as I vaulted over the deck railing with my archers and we started running towards the gate in the city wall gate in front of us.

As I ran towards the gate, I looked back over my shoulder and could see some of our boarding parties running along the quay to the Moorish galleys and cargo transports on our left and other boarding parties running to the Moorish galleys and cargo transports on our right. The vessels moored in the berths along the quay are packed close together one right after the next so our prize crews didn't have far to go. They were running hard and reached them and leapt aboard their intended prizes in what seemed like the blink of an eye.

I started in the lead and was running hard, but some of my archers were beginning to catch up with me and move ahead. One of them who had gotten ahead of me stopped and began loosing arrows. As I came past him I heard his rhythmic chant of "notch and push" followed by a grunt as he launched at the handful of Tunisians standing in front of the open gate.

Even as I ran I was aware of the shouting and commotion both on the quay behind me and on the ships behind us moored to the quay. The next time I looked back, I could see Jeffrey standing there alone on his deck, right where he should be, ready to give whatever orders are necessary to his crew and the men on his section of the quay.

****** *Harold*

We closed with a possible prize in the harbour whilst out of the corner of my eye I watched the galleys led by William and Peter approach the quay. So far, so good — we seem to have caught the heathen bastards by surprise.

"Archers, cease rowing and come on deck. Steer to the big one over there," I shouted to the sailor sergeant as the rowing drum began to slow its beat.

"Yes. The big one, the one with two masts and all the square sails. Steer for it.... Hurry, damn you, hurry."

Then I stood on the roof of the forward castle and rocked back and forth and said nothing for a few minutes until we approached the big two-masted cog. It was anchored and quiet.

"Grapplers, archers, and number three boarding party men to the deck. Grapplers, archers, and number three boarding party to the deck. Get ready, lads. Here comes more coins for us all. Throw your grapples as she comes.

"Throw. Throw. Stand by with the tow line."

The transport I had us going after was one of the biggest two-masted cogs I'd ever seen. Two tall masts, square sails, no oars, and a strange flag with strange markings.

Wonder where it's from? Well, I guess we're about to find out.

"Who's cog is that, Harold?" my pilot asked as we watched our boarding party climb their ladders. "I've never seen a flag like that before."

"First time for me too, by God? Ninety paces long if she's a foot. I think she's one of those new heathen ships the goddamn Moors began using after they catched me up as a slave.

"I saw a couple of ships with the same flag; at least, I think it was the same. In Acre, it was. . . . When the Saracens held the castle and the Moors was welcome and I was rowing on the lower bench. Square sails, they had, and two masts.... Not as big as this one though."

"Stand by to throw the climbing ropes and grapples. Stand by, lads. Throw. Throw."

"No one on deck," was the welcome cry from one of the two archers in the lookout's little nest on our mast.

It changed to, "Here, they come," few seconds after our grapples were thrown and began to hook on to the cog. Then the archers in the nest began launching their arrows and I could hear shouting in a strange tongue coming from the cog's deck. *Well, the heathens are obviously on the deck now.*

Our prize men were just starting to climb the grapple rope ladders with swords and bows slung on their backs when there was another grunt and a scream above us and then a hail from the mast.

"The deck's clear. They've run below. We got a couple of the bastards. The rest have run. Some in the stern castle, for sure."

Our prize crew sailors and their two archers went hand over hand up the knotted grappling lines in a hurry and disappeared over the cog's rail. Less than a minute later, a face looked down at us and the sergeant of the prize crew shouted to me in an elated voice.

"We've taken it." *Of course, he's elated; he'll be its sergeant captain and put up another stripe if he can get it to Malta.*

"Good luck," I shouted back with a wave and a raised thumb. No time to waste, I was already looking for our next prize.

"Go for that one next," I yelled into the ear of the sailor sergeant standing next to me as I pointed to a cog at anchor nearby. It was smaller cog with a single mast.

"Grapplers and boarding party number two stand by."

Chapter Twelve

William enters Tunis.

My archers and I were sweating heavily under the glaring midday sun as we left the quay and began lumbering towards the city gate carrying our longbows. It was a hard slog because we were all labouring under the weight of the half dozen or so leather quivers full of arrows each of us had slung over his back, as many as each man could carry.

As we got closer to the gate, a couple of the archers in front of me stopped running and began launching arrows at the men still around the gate and on the ramparts above it. Others apparently thought it's what they were supposed to do and stopped to join them.

"Don't stop. Don't stop," I croaked out with a gasp as I ran past them. "Get to the gate. To the gate, lads. Run. Run."

So far the wind looks to be somewhat favourable. Our fear, Harold's and mine, is the wind will shift so some of our men will be trapped in the harbour on their prizes and unable to leave because they don't have enough sailors to work their sails. It's a concern because we are going to try to take off the Moors' sailing ships as well as their galleys. How long we'll have to hold the city gates to keep the Moors away from the sailing ships in the harbour and the galleys beached along the shore depends on the wind.

Within a few minutes we reached the city gate and sprinted into the little square beyond it. The gate was open, and the area around it deserted except for a couple of dead and wounded Moors, the men who went down from our archers' brief spurt of shooting as we ran.

Most of the people we'd seen standing around in front of the city gate disappeared when our initial burst of arrows began falling. To our surprise, there were still a few unarmed men and women standing around in the open area immediately inside the gate—they gaped at us in disbelief as we ran in. But they quickly disappeared.

Even before I could catch my breath, I began shouting orders to the archers who've beaten me into the little square—they'd gotten inside the gate and just stopped because they didn't know what to do next.

"Get up those stairs; take the gatehouse and clear the walls in both directions. Hurry, all of you. Run. Run."

Before I could even finish giving my first order, there were literally a hundred or more wild-eyed and panting archers in the open space inside the gate. The sun was so scorching they were soon huddled against the buildings and the wall seeking shade—and several doors were quickly broken down so the men could shelter inside out of the sun.

I thought to myself that it was good thing there were so many of us because streets and alleys ran in various directions from the little square inside the gate and along the city wall. We needed to block them all. There was not a moment to lose.

"Sergeant," I shouted at an older archer whose name I suddenly couldn't remember, "take your men and go down there to the next wall tower and hold it. Hurry, man. Run, damn it, run."

In less than a minute, I had reinforcements dashing up the stairs to help clear more of the ramparts on the wall and groups of men pounding down the various streets and alleys to set up blocking positions at the first intersection they reach.

"Clear the wall in both directions all the way down to the next gate in the city wall—and beyond if you can," I told the sergeant who promptly led his men in a rush up the stone stairs next to the gatehouse.

I kept about thirty archers in the little square to be a rapid reaction force I can send to wherever their longbows might be needed most.

Damn, it would have been helpful if we'd had a map of this place before we came through the gate.

"Sergeant, send your strongest runner down the outside of the wall to see if we've taken the other city gate in front of the quay."

****** *William*

An hour later and things seemed to be falling into place. Tunis was strangely silent and we controlled most of the city wall in front of the harbour. From the top of the gatehouse, I watched more and more galleys and sailing ships leave the harbour. I knew they're prizes because some of them were being towed. And I knew when Henry was finished on the beach because I could see the last of his archers running back to one of our galleys and climbing back aboard.

A runner arrived from Peter with an update. The city gate he had tried to reach was closed by the time he and his men reached it. But he has it now because some of my men who climbed the steps next to the gate I entered were able to come across along the unguarded ramparts on top of city walls to Peter's gate. They ran off the men who had closed it and opened it from the inside.

Peter also reported an increasing amount of activity in the tent encampment and livestock markets along the river. He didn't know what it meant so he decided to hold only the gate and the wall above it; he said he was going to keep a large part of his force outside the city wall so he would be able to block a counter-attack coming through the open area between the encampment and the harbour, an attack that might trap some of his men inside the city.

"Good decision," was the message I send back with Peter's huffing and puffing runner. "Protecting our men on the quay and in the harbour is more important than taking the city."

Amidst the turmoil and confusion, I could see some of our galleys and even more of what were obviously prizes rowing for the harbour entrance. Others had already passed through the entrance and were disappearing into the distance towards the horizon. Clouds of black smoke were starting to come from a couple of galleys on the beach.

Damn; those galleys must not have had slaves on their rowing benches or been pulled too far up on the beach to be gotten off and towed.

I could also see puffs of smoke coming from one of the galleys anchored in the harbour next to where some of Long Bob's men appeared to be boarding a cog.

I knew it was Bob and his men because his galley had such a unique sail; I wondered why he decided to burn the Tunisian instead of towing it out?

Despite the burning hot sun there was activity all along the beach and in the harbour. It was like a wasp's nest that has been overturned. Worse, the wind seems to have died and there was a great deal of activity on two or three of the ships in the harbour. Even from here I can see people massing on their decks. They may be there to repel our boarders.

Damn. They must be newly arrived and didn't have time to unload their men in time for them to attend the prayers in the mosque. Or could they be Venetians or Genoese or Jews?

****** *Sergeant Captain Edward Fiennes*

I could see men on the quay and Harold's galley sending a boarding party on to a cog off to our right as we rowed closer to the two-masted

Moorish cargo cog I've set my eyes on. That's when the archers up in the lookout's nest on my mast shouted down to report the Moor's deck is crowded with armed men.

"They've got swords and shields," one of the archers shouted. "More than twenty men; maybe thirty."

Suddenly, both of our archers in the lookout's nest shouted warnings at the same time and began shooting arrows as fast as they could loose them.

"They've got archers, by God. Archers."

We no more than hear the warning of the men in the lookout's nest when one of the archers in the lookout's nest suddenly slumped back against the ropes and his bow dropped to the deck. Then fist-sized rocks started coming down around us. *Damnation. They've got slingers too.*

One of our would-be grapplers suddenly dropped like he'd been axed as we veered off and slid past the bow of the big cog. Then a rock barely missed me, and another of our grapplers staggered and sat down on the deck with an arrow in his chest.

When I looked up at the mast again, I could see that neither of our archers were in action; one had obviously been hit and was sitting slumped with both arms over the safety ropes to keep from falling; the other was trying to shelter behind the mast. *Damn. Those Moorish bastards up there are dangerous.*

"Don't throw," I screamed at the sailors who were winding up to throw with the grapples they were swinging around and around over their heads. "Don't throw, goddamn it. We'll pass this one. Steer to that one. Yes, that's the one."

Then from behind me, there were screams of warning. One of the galley's we'd taken as a prize was coming straight at us with a cog in tow. Behind it I could see other galleys, clearly prizes, rowing for the harbour entrance.

"Brace yourself."

I shouted my warning just before the bow of the oncoming galley sliced into the side of my galley. Wood and other debris flew across our deck as it impaled us. *I knew I should have learnt to swim.*

****** *William*

The view from up here on the city wall was spectacular. I could see the entire Tunis harbour and the beach around it. It was less crowded with ships than when I looked an hour ago.

Similarly, the shoreline where the Moorish galleys were beached is now almost empty of galleys—an open area in front of it is rapidly filling with townspeople. *Wonder where they came from? There must be another gate in the city wall on that side.*

So far, so good—all of the galleys which landed us are still waiting at the quay to take us off when we are finished here.

Also good is that some of our crews with galleys from the beach seem to be moving them into the harbour. I think Henry's lads are trying to find cogs to tow away. Good on them.

My God, I hope we have enough coins in Cyprus for all the prize money I've promised the men.

Uh oh. There's trouble. Damn, a collision. It looks like one of the galleys in the harbour is sinking. I hope it's not one of ours. *Well, there's nothing I can do from up here; Harold will have to sort it out.*

Suddenly, a shout from down at the foot of the stone stairs jerked my attention away from the scene in the harbour.

"Captain, Captain. Please, Captain." Roger said to tell you his men are being attacked on the lane leading up to the street along the city wall; he thinks he can hold them but he needs more arrows."

I went down the stairs two at a time. It was very warm, and as I ran down the stairs, I suddenly felt very light headed; we'll have to find something to drink if we stay here much longer.

"Follow me," I shouted to the archers in the shade along the wall as I started running up the lane towards Roger and his men.

The archers fell in behind me and we pounded over the street stone towards where Roger was last located. it didn't take long before we could hear the unmistakable sound of fighting ahead of us where the wall curves—and met a couple of wounded archers trying to make their back to the city gate.

One of the archers seemed to be badly hurt and was being helped along by the other who was bleeding from a head wound but otherwise seemed quite fit. I rushed on past them without asking who they are or how it happened.

A moment later, I came to one of our men all white faced and asleep on the street in the sun.

"Help him back to the galley," I gasped at the man running next to me.

Ahead of me I could see Roger and his men standing on either side of an open area where a lane runs into the street I was running on—and to reach them I had to get past two more of our men—one was on the ground sleeping and the other was struggling to stand up. *What's wrong here?*

"Roger, what's the situation?" I gasped as I

reached him. "What happened to your men and why are they taking off their tunics?" That's what I blurted out as I rushed up to my sergeant.

"There are Moorish soldiers up this lane. We've been keeping them back with our arrows, but it looks like they're forming up to rush us again."

"And your butcher's bill?"

"All from the heat. We've got no water." *Of course. That explains why some of Roger's men have taken off their tunics.*

"Right. Tell your lads it's alright to take off some of their clothes if they're too hot. Tell them it's alright if they have to leave them when we pull back. We'll outfit them from our stores when we're back on our ships."

Less than ten minutes later I decided to pull Roger's men back. There were a lot of clothes on the ground when we start backing up towards the city gate — including my pants and shirt. All I was wearing was my tunic with the seven black stripes signifying I was the captain.

There is no doubt about it; we should have been carrying water skins instead of so many quivers.

Chapter Thirteen

We abandon the city.

We'd held the gates for a couple of hours, and the harbour and beach were emptying out. It was time to go. So I sent runners along the top of the city walls and down every street and lane with orders for the sergeants to have everyone fall back to the city gate.

"Tell them to walk their archers back to the city gate and to maintain order when they do — and not to leave a single man or body behind. It will be their heads if they leave anyone behind."

Whilst the runners were off carrying my message, I climbed the stairs to once again look at the harbour and the beach. Things looked good. Henry's archers were off the beach and the harbour was almost empty. There were outward bound galleys and cogs on the water beyond the harbour entrance. It was almost time to fall back to the quay and board our galleys.

Any thoughts I might have had about holding the city were long gone. I realised it would be impossible as soon as I saw the Caliph's great fortress beyond the city walls and the open areas all around it.

Within minutes, groups of hot and sweaty archers began coming into the square and taking up positions to block its various entrances. More than a few of them had to be helped and our dead and sleeping men were being carried. The heat was taking a terrible toll.

"Sergeants, form up your men and call your rolls to see if anyone is missing and unaccounted for. It's on every man's head if even one of his mates is left behind." *I care and I want the men to know I care.*

"Guy, take your entire company and escort our wounded and heat struck men to the quay and get them loaded. And watch out for the Moors who are starting to gather on the beach where the Moors had their galleys. They're probably curiosity seekers but don't take any chances; tell your men to shoot at anyone who gets in range."

They don't look organised; probably just lookers who are curious about what happened. But you never know, do you?

Once again I nipped up the stairs to have a look from the ramparts on top of the gate house. I needed to make sure Peter had gotten the word to withdraw. We wouldn't stop blocking this gate until his main force was on its way to the quay. He should be getting the word about now if my messenger got through.

The archers who were up on the wall will know if he did. And even if he didn't, Peter will see Guy's men moving down to the quay and know it means we're pulling out.

"Where are the sergeants who were on the wall towards the other gate?" I shouted. "Are the men at the other gate pulling back?"

******

We ran for the quay after one last look around to make sure no one had been left behind. Ahead of us I could see our men reaching the quay and boarding their galleys. I could also see what was obviously Peter's rearguard hurrying towards the quay.

The heat was unbearable. The first thing every man is going to do when he gets on board, including me, is head straight for the water barrel and one of the dipping bowls.

As I climbed on board, I could see a number of men stretched out on the deck and rowing benches being tended to by their mates and Helen. They were being given bowls of drinking water and breakfast ale. Hastily rigged sails were helping shade them from the sun.

A distressed and harried-looking Helen saw me on the quay and came hurrying over to the deck railing. She handed me a little water skin as I climbed on board and I gave her a brief, one-armed hug — then I took a quick couple of swallows and climbed part way up the galley mast towards the lookout's nest to see what I could see.

A group of fifty or sixty of Peter's men were walking together backwards towards the quay. A large number that had already arrived were actively boarding their galleys. The walkers must be Peter and his rear guard.

There was a great mob of Moors following along behind Peter's rear guard, but they are certainly keeping their distance and appeared to be more of a disorganised mob of curious men and boys than a threat.

The city gate Peter occupied was closed again, so most of the people following Peter must be from the caravanserais and tents next to the river up by the livestock market.

Hmm. I wonder who closed the city gate and why? I'll have to ask Peter when I see him. Probably a case of closing the barn door after the ox got out.

******

There. Finally. I could see Peter's galley begin to move away from the quay and its oars go into the water. That's the last one.

"Push off, Jeffrey. It's time to go."

Chapter Fourteen

We beat a retreat.

"Hoist the 'follow me' flag and get underway," I ordered Jeffrey in a voice loud enough for his rudder man and drummer to hear.

"Then have your loud-talker hail the other two galleys and tell them to follow us. Tell them we're going to go through the harbour, and check the galleys and transports still there to make sure all of our people have gotten clear."

I particularly want to check on the galley that looked as if it was sinking. I think it was one of ours, Long Bob's I'm almost certain. I wonder what happened. And, of course, I once again want our sergeants and men to know that we are determined not to leave anyone behind.

Less than a minute later the rowing drum began slowly beating its monotonous cadence, and we pulled away from the quay. Helen was next to me holding out a mug of ships' water into which she had squeezed a lemon she had found in the Lisbon market. *It's something she learnt from her mother; she says it's even more cooling than ale.*

We were almost immediately among the handful of boats still in the harbour. Several of them were clearly still in the hands of the Moors — but not many, and most of those which were here when we arrived are gone.

"Hoy the deck," came the warning cry from the mast. "The big one dead ahead has men on the deck wearing turbans. They're armed."

I don't know what made me think of it, but an idea popped into my mind from what the Saracens did at Edmund's castle years ago.

"Helen, please run to our forecastle and get my bow and a couple of arrows — the longest ones you can find; and bring all the linen strips we use for our arses if they're clean and dry.

"Jeffrey, please tell the sailor cook to light a cooking fire and send a man to bring me a big armful of the cook's driest and smallest firewood kindling." *Fire arrows, by God; maybe we can burn the bastard if we can't take it.*

Jeffrey's men rowed us on past the Moorish ship so we could look over the last few ships still in the harbour whilst he and the rest of his crew rushed around trying to organise fire arrows.

All we found were a couple of our prizes, galleys from the beach with Henry's men on board—which each had an empty sailing ship in tow and were rowing hard to slowly pull it out of the harbour.

The only other ships still in the harbour were two single-masted sailing ships with Moorish crews and the Moorish cog we passed a few minutes ago. They been passed for one reason or another—probably because they showed fight and there were easier pickings elsewhere. I'll have to ask Harold when I see him.

There was no telling how many Moorish ships, if any, raised their sails and successfully left when our prize crews began taking prizes from among those not strong enough to resist; or what we could have done to stop them.

We also found a listing and abandoned prize galley with a badly damaged bow and a couple of dead Moors on its lower rowing deck, but no trace of whatever it had hit. The chains of its slave rowers are still on the rowing benches but they're empty; the slaves and other survivors must have been picked up by Harold or one of his galleys.

It was time to leave. The two galleys following us swung around when we did and followed us as we once again rowed past the three Moorish ships still in the harbour. The Moorish captains must have changed their minds about staying in the harbour and fighting off boarders; by the time we got back to them, they'd all three raised their anchors and were setting their sails to leave. *Hopefully, they're getting under way too late.*

They weren't too late. Our fire arrows didn't work. We easily shot them into the Moors' wooden hulls as we rowed past — but the flames either went out while they were flying through the air or the bundles of rags and kindling wood fell apart before their hulls could catch fire. All we ended up doing was wasting time and giving the Moors a good scare.

****** *William*

Our plans changed. Except for one of our prize galleys and the cog it was slowly towing, there were no more Moorish galleys in the harbour or nosed into the shore. That was important; it meant there was no need for Jeffrey and the captains of our two sister galleys to stop at the entrance to block it whilst our galleys and prizes escape.

Even so, our drum went silent and we stopped rowing when we reached the harbour entrance. A few minutes later, the last of our prizes rows slowly rowed past us towing an unmanned Moorish cog. The sound of its rowing drum and the voices came over the water as it slid past us.

Spirits were high and the handful of men on our decks gave each other cheers and waves as the prize galley and its tow slowly slide past. It's little wonder the prize galley's deck is so empty; our prize crews are small so almost every man is where he should be — at a rudder or oar to help the slaves on the rowing benches. Everyone on board wanted to get out of the harbour at the highest possible speed, however slow that might be — it was exactly what they should be doing.

It will be a while before the prize galley and its tow will be over the horizon towards the south and out of sight of any pursuers we might have missed. We'll stay here just in case until they are almost out of sight. Then we'll catch up with them and escort them to Malta. But then I had a thought.

"Jeffrey, do any of your men have experience on sailing ships?"

We came alongside the towed cog and boarded a dozen sailors and archers to help crew her. Then we moved away and watched whilst our two sister galleys convoyed two prize galleys out of the harbour, the final two prizes and the last of our galleys.

It was time to go.

******

Jeffrey had us moving nicely using both our sail and oars when the lookout on the mast reported a galley dead in the water off our port bow. A few seconds later, as soon as its crew could see us from their deck, the galley's rowing drum started and some of its oars began to row—and some of them keep rowing even after we came alongside and hailed it with an order it to stop and be boarded.

"Come down immediately," I shouted up to the sailor in the lookout's nest. "I'm sending up archers.

"Jeffrey, get your two best archers up there with their bows."

Less than a minute later the lookout was on the deck and a couple of archers were in the lookout's nest with their longbows and quivers of arrows.

"Can you see the man at the rudder or the rowing drum?" I shouted up to the archers as they scramble up the mast.

"If you can see either of them, take them."

******

It was totally dark, and the warm and sunny day had turned into a rather nice but windy evening by the time we cast off the grappling lines from the prize galley we had recaptured; our new prize crew and the Tunisian's slaves were once again rowing our recaptured prize towards Malta.

The only difference was that now twenty of Jeffrey's archers were on board to keep order and help row—and Jeffrey's galley was seriously short of rowers.

According to the last report about the recaptured prize, all of the Tunisian slaves except the most seriously wounded were once again chained to the lower rowing benches. They were wolfing down bread and cheese from the food we hurriedly passed over to the prize whilst it was still light enough to see what we were doing.

All we know for sure is that two men of the ten men in our original prize crew have been killed and five wounded, one quite seriously. We'll sort out the slaves and what happened when we reach Malta and Harold can talk to what's left of the men in our prize crew. *Our three unwounded survivors are still on board so I rather doubt the leader or leaders of the mutiny will reach Malta.*

Chapter Fifteen

The rendezvous in Malta

Helen and I were standing side by side at the very front of Jeffrey's galley as we slowly rowed into Malta's harbour late the next day. It was a moment to savour despite the oppressive heat, and I certainly do — the harbour was packed with ships and we rowed between them towards the quay to an increasingly enthusiastic reception as the word spread of our arrival and their sailors and archers poured on to their decks to cheer and wave.

Most of the galleys and sailing ships in the harbour, it seems, were ours and most of them were prizes. There was also no doubt about it — their cheering and waving sailors and archers were pleased and happy. They should be; we'll be passing out a huge amount of prize money when we reach Cyprus, and rightly so.

Malta's old stone quay was teeming with all kinds of activity. Men and carts and merchants and curious citizens were everywhere. Harold, Henry, and a number of our most senior sergeants were all waiting with big smiles and open arms as we bumped up against the quay and willing hands tied us up at the one and only space our galleys had not already taken. It had been cleared, I later found out, and was waiting for us.

There was a huge crowd of our men and curious local citizens standing in a great half circle behind the senior sergeants to welcome us. *And, thank God, there's Long Bob; Harold or one his galleys must have picked him up when his galley went down. He'll have a story to tell for sure. I wonder what happened.*

We English have a reputation for being staid and stoic and not showing much emotion. But you wouldn't know it from the great hugs and back slapping and cheers that began when I stepped from the roof of the forecastle and Harold pulled me up on to the quay by my extended arm. The men were pleased and there was no halfway about it. I was damned pleased myself.

Helen was still standing demurely on the forecastle roof when I turned back and Henry and I each took one of Helen's arms and pulled her up to join us. It made me laugh out loud in delight, and a very pleased Helen smiled shyly, when each of the bearded ruffians very carefully bent down and took her hand and kissed it.

They all knew she was with me and must have planned it; however they did it, it warmed my heart almost to tears and so did the cheers of the crowd gathering around us. It was all I could do to flutter my hands at the crowd around us and mouth my thanks as I nodded my appreciation to them.

****** *William*

A few minutes later a great crowd followed us as we walked arm in arm down to the tavern just off the end of the quay. It's the same place where I first met Count Brindisi, the old pirate who is now Malta's lord.

"We knew we'd need a place to meet with our captains so we clubbed together and rented the whole tavern as soon as we got here this morning," Peter explained as he stepped around a milky-eyed beggar sitting cross-legged on the quay with his hand outstretched.

"I wager we've taken more prizes than anyone has ever taken before, maybe ever," Harold exclaimed at the same time. "It's unbelievable; it really is."

"What's the latest count?" asked Henry to no one in particular.

"At least sixty have come in so far, maybe more; we really won't know for sure for at least a week."

"Yoram will get weak knees and faint," I offered with a big laugh that got smiling nods from everyone, "from all the prize money we'll have to hand out."

Moments later we beamed big smiles and cheerful greetings to a file of archers guarding the tavern's entrance and duck our heads to enter the smoke-filled room. It was deserted except for its smiling owner and his wife. And it was empty even though there are a lot of thirsty men in town.

Peter must have put a guard on the door as soon as he rented it. Smart move; we're going to need someplace private where we can talk to our sergeant captains and make our lists.

"Taking this place was a smart move, Peter. Thank you."

But then I got to thinking.

"Harold, before we sit down and have a drink and hear how Bob Long learnt to swim and who fished him out, don't you think we should make arrangements to keep order in the city tonight? Our men are rightly going to be celebrating tonight and they're likely to cause trouble if we're not careful—we don't want to shite where we walk; we may want to call in here again sometime."

The response I get from Henry put a smile on my face.

"We're way ahead of you, William. Brindisi has already ordered all the taverns and whorehouses in the city to close at sundown tonight. He said to tell you hello, by the way, and to tell you he'd like to lift a mug with you before we leave."

******

We drank and ate and told stories of what we'd done and what we'd seen until late that evening. Along the way, we reached a number of decisions. One of the most important was that we must immediately outfit our men in hot weather clothes and find some way to tell their ranks from looking at them.

Another was that starting tomorrow morning every regular sergeant captain and prize sergeant was to come here and report on the size of his crew and who is in it. *It was almost certain that we would have to take men from some of our galleys and prizes and put them on others if we were to get all our prizes to Cyprus.*

"Having so many prizes is wonderful; the men were wonderful," I drunkenly announced with a great deal of satisfaction for about the tenth time.

"But it means we now have so many galleys and cogs and men we'll never be able to remember them all, not me at least, especially when I'm drunk. So we'll have to make a list if we're to know who needs what — and I'm the only one who knows how to scribe and we have no parchments and inks."

Finally, I staggered my way up the narrow staircase to a sleeping room with Helen holding my arm and carrying a candle lantern to make sure I didn't fall and hurt myself. *It had been a great day.*

"It's been a great day, hasn't it, Helen?"

****** *William*

Everything was confusion the next morning when the sun came up and we reassembled around one of the tavern's tables for a bowl of breakfast ale and some fresh bread and cheese from the tavern owner's wife. We needed to finish talking about we should do next.

It took a while but we finally resolved two of the big issues that faced us — what to do with the many hundreds of newly freed galley slaves and how to provision and man our prizes so they have a reasonable chance to get to Cyprus.

The slaves were an easy decision. We need them to help row our prizes to Cyprus. So Harold and Henry immediately went to the quay to spread the word that Malta doesn't want them and will return them to slavery if they go ashore here. They were to tell every sergeant that unless a slave is originally from Malta, he can't go ashore until we reach our base in Cyprus.

"Tell the slaves they'll be free once we reach Cyprus. Then they can do whatever they want including staying with us and working for us for their food and drink. But until then, they're staying on board for their own safety and in chains for our safety, unless they are British or French, of course."

It's not true about Malta returning them to slavery; at least I don't think so. But one never knows with an old pirate like Brindisi who uses slaves to row his galleys.

It took a couple of hours, but Harold and Henry and Peter finally returned from making the rounds of our prizes and we were able begin talking with the sergeants gathering outside.

We were listening to Alfred, the prize sergeant of what he enthusiastically describes as a fine, Tunisian, eighty-oar galley, when one of

Peter's sergeants knocked on the open wooden door to get our attention and bustled in.

Alfred obviously wants us to keep the prize with him in command, so I suspect he would be describing it as a fine galley even if it was riddled with worms and sinking out from under him. Good on him; I would expect nothing less.

The interruption by Peter's sergeant was more than welcome because he'd brought some of the things we need most — ground charcoal for ink and blank parchments and, best of all, one of the city's public scribes, a rotund, old greybeard who usually sits in the city square reading and writing petitions and agreements and letters and such for the people who can't read or scribe.

Two minutes of conversation and it was clear the old man can read and scribe in Latin, Italian, and French; he was a welcome sight for the sore eyes in my aching head.

"Please sit here on the bench right next to me. I want you to assist me in the writing of some lists. I'll tell you when and what to write."

Damn it. It can't be helped, but he's going to know our strength and problems. We'll either have to kill him or take him with us.

We worked right on through our afternoon meal until the sun finished passing overhead and darkness began to fall. It took many hours, but by the end of the day we had a list of all of our galleys and prizes which had reached Malta. And on the list was the name of each ship's sergeant captain and information about the size and nature of its crew and supplies.

As we expected, some of our ships have enough supplies and men to reach Cyprus; others clearly do not. The prize galleys, in particular, are seriously short of having enough food and water. Some of the prizes had none on board when they left Tunis and their prize crews and slaves suffered greatly before they got here.

Food and supplies were a major problem, particularly since we need to put the slaves on double or triple rations to strengthen them up. It was something we'd have to solve before we leave. And solving it was certainly going to make the local merchants rich and Brindisi happy with all the taxes he'll take off of them.

Some of the Tunisian prizes may not have enough archers on board to prevent crew and slave mutinies after the sail for Cyprus. We've already had one that we know of and that's enough. Harold and Henry and Peter will be dealing with that as well—we're going to spread our archers out so that every prize will have at least a sergeant and two files of archers on board between here and Cyprus in addition to its prize captain and his crew of sailors. The archers can help row when they're needed.

******

Three days later, the wind was favourable and an English armada of over sixty galleys and cogs left Malta bound for Cyprus — forty-nine war galleys, fourteen cargo cogs, and over thirteen hundred fully trained archers.

We had so many cargo cogs sailing with us because some of them aren't ours — two days ago the local merchants sent a delegation asking for permission for some of their cogs and ships to sail with our fleet. The merchants were very clear as to why they were making the request — they want to decrease the likelihood their ships will be taken by pirates.

"Every pirate knows that attacking an English galley or cog almost certainly means death and the loss of his galley," one of the merchants assured me.

Not everyone was going. Peter would stay behind in the port with two galleys for a few more days in case any of the three missing prizes come in. He'll keep a large complement of archers with him so they can serve on the missing galleys — if they come in.

Also staying behind were two prize galleys that appeared to be in need of extensive repairs to make them seaworthy. Peter will look into the alternatives and make a decision about each of them. Their anxious prize captains and their crews will stay with them. *Of course, the two prize captains and sergeants are anxious. They've got to get their galleys to Cyprus to have their promotions confirmed.*

I personally went to the archers and galley crewmen staying behind to assure them they will get their full share of the prize money. I even advanced them some coins so they could enjoy their stay. *The slaves from the two galleys were also pleased. They were immediately released after being told a useful lie – that if they run the Maltese will return them to slavery.*

The chubby, old greybeard who helped me as a scribe turned out not to be a problem. His name is Angelo del Gato and he jumped at the chance of going to Cyprus with us to work as a scribe either there or wherever else we might need him.

"Malta is very small, and I have been here for many years; I'd like to see more of the world before I die."

Angelo didn't admit it, but since he knew both Latin and how to scribe I suspect he's a former priest who ran afoul of the Church. If he is, it's actually a strong recommendation in these days of church-sponsored corruption and massacres.

What's really strange is that we also have another Angelo who used to be a priest and knows how to scribe. He's in Cornwall helping Thomas put learning on the boys. I wonder if that's a name priests adopt when they leave the Church? I'll have to ask Thomas; he knows about such things.

Chapter Sixteen

William gets a surprise.

Cyprus was in sight, and Helen was so excited I thought she was going to burst. She's been anxious to see her best friend, Yoram's wife Lena, ever since we left Cornwall. For the past week or so almost all she has talked about is seeing Lena again and how her baby girl must have grown and whether the new baby Lena was expecting when we left for England last year turned out to be a boy or a girl. Well, she's just about to find out — we're passing through the harbour entrance and the Limassol quay is dead ahead.

A number of our galleys have already arrived and I could see a couple of the cogs anchored in the harbour that I recognised as being some of our prizes.

******

Our early-arriving galleys alerted everyone about our huge victory in Tunis and all the prizes we took. They also reported that Henry, Helen, and I were on Harold's galley and would be arriving soon.

It's no wonder, then, that Yoram and Lena, and Brian and Samuel Farmer and many others are all waiting with big smiles as Harold shouted out the orders to ease our galley up to the quay and our rowing drum stopped beating.

Albert, Thomas Cook, and William Chester are standing there with them. I wonder who else has already made it to Cyprus? And there, by God, are Aaron and Reuben.

"Hello, hello," I shouted as I stepped over the railing and began greeting my old friends with handshakes and back slapping hugs. Out of the corner of my eye, I could see Harold and one of his sailors helping a tearfully happy Helen over the rail and into the arms of an equally tearful and happy Lena. *I didn't realise they'd become such good friends.*

It was total chaos on the crowded quay as the sun begins setting in the distance; happy chaos. There was much to talk about and everyone was talking at the same time about everything as we slowly walked around the city walls to the old fortified farmhouse we'd turned into an impressive and fearsome citadel.

******

Yoram laid on a big dinner with Lena and Helen and all of our senior sergeants—all the original archers who are in port were here along with Yoram, Harold, Peter, and Yoram's assistant, and Andy Anderson. Joseph, Harold's second, was also present in case anyone wanted to know about our ships and sailors already here in the Holy Land waters. Indeed, so many people came to the dinner we ate outside in the innermost of our three baileys because we couldn't all fit into the downstairs room. *If Yoram and the others say Joseph did a good job of standing in for Harold, we'll make him a senior sergeant as well.*

Finally, Lena whispered in Yoram's ear and he shooed everyone to their quarters, so Helen and I could get some sleep after an exhausting day. We'll be sleeping once again in the old farmhouse's downstairs room where the senior sergeants used to sleep. Lena and Yoram are in the upstairs room with the coin chests.

"Don't worry about the sergeants," Yoram assured me as the last of them went cheerfully out the gate and into the middle bailey.

"Over the winter we used logs from the

King's forest to build a wooden defensive wall dividing the middle bailey in half — and then built rooms for the senior sergeants in one half and for the other sergeants in the other. They're living like kings."

******

Helen obviously enjoyed being here. The next morning, she was singing to herself and smiling as she traipsed up the stairs to be with Lena so Yoram and I can meet privately to discuss the state of our coins before the sergeants arrive for today's meetings.

The coin situation in our chests upstairs is, in a word, splendid — coins have continued to pour in from our refugee carrying and other operations. The number of coins we have in our chests upstairs is quite staggering. It's a king's ransom second only to coins we have in Cornwall and more come in every time a galley arrives or departs with more refugees and parchments.

I didn't say a word to anyone, not even Yoram, but I was greatly relieved. In a couple of days, we'll have to pay out a huge amount of prize money for the unexpectedly large number of prizes we took out of Tunis. The prizes are still coming in so we don't yet know exactly how much we'll be paying out to our men, only that it will be well over two thousand bezants because we took so many prizes.

To my surprise, Yoram reported we were now earning almost as much from the merchants and others using our rapidly growing coin transfer and protection services as we were carrying pilgrims and refugees.

"Word has spread through the merchant communities that we can be trusted," Yoram explained.

"Many of the merchants who gave us a try liked the results, and then others heard about it from the merchants and their friends. They are using our parchment orders more and more instead of taking the risk of sending actual coins back and forth using their own couriers."

Then Yoram said something that knocked me out of my sandals whilst we waited for the other sergeants to arrive.

"Congratulations, by the way; Lena told me about the new baby last night."

"What new baby?"

******

I ran up the stairs two at a time and was still in a state of shocked elation when the sergeants began arriving a few minutes later for today's meeting.

We sat around the big table in the hall with bowls of breakfast ale and talked about many things. *Though I must admit I didn't listen as carefully as I should; I was more than a bit distracted by the news that I'm going to be a father again.*

First and foremost, we agreed to immediately announce the initial prize monies for the Tunis prizes would be given out in four days. Waiting four days will give more of our prizes a chance to reach Limassol and increase each man's initial payout. There will be a second payout for late-arriving prizes in thirty days.

Any sooner, and the men will think we are trying to avoid paying them for some of the prizes; any later, and they'll start worrying that we are trying to avoid paying altogether.

Once the timing of the prize money payments was settled, we had a long discussion about the clothes our men are wearing and the difficulties of knowing friend from foe in the midst of a battle, to say nothing of knowing one man's rank from another man's when we are going about our daily chores. Everyone seemed to have at least one experience they wanted to share.

There was also total agreement about the clothes the men are bringing from England being too warm for working or fighting in the summer heat. Those who hadn't been at the Tunis walls laughed when Peter and I described how we and our men had taken our tunics, pants, and shirts off in Tunis in order to fight naked in the excruciating heat; they were shocked and stopped laughing when they heard about our men collapsing and two of them dying.

Everyone nodded emphatically when I said, "Never again; we must get proper clothes for our men."

Yoram suggested an answer. He thinks in the summer we should use the brownish linen gowns and woven straw hats the Egyptians wear when they have to be outside in the summer. Then we'll know our men because they'll all be in the colour gowns and have the same hats. He thinks they are so common we'd be able to immediately buy the three thousand we'd need.

My God, do we really have three thousand men? The number startled us all even if it did include spares.

After much discussion, I told Yoram to buy the summer gowns and hats and get them to the men as quickly as possible—we'll pay for the first one for every man including the slaves we release; they'll be responsible for replacing them when they wear out or get lost, except for work or battle damage, of course.

The gowns are to be in sizes large enough so when the weather is cold they can be worn over the archers' warmer clothes from England — and when we get them, we'll have the men sew stripes or ribbons on the front and back of their gowns so everyone will know each man's rank as soon as he sees his stripes: none for freed slaves, workers, apprentice archers and pike men; one for archers fully trained as marines; two for chosen men; three for sergeants; four for sergeant captains, and so on and so on all the way up to seven for me as the captain; six for Thomas, Yoram, Henry, Harold, and Peter as my lieutenants; and five for the senior sergeants.

It was starting to get uncomfortably warm, and it was all I could do to keep awake by the time Yoram began a long report on the state of our galley operations and about starting construction here in Limassol to further strengthen our fortress — a fourth curtain wall and bailey and internal walls to divide the outer baileys.

Yoram also wants us to consider using some of our new prizes to start additional sailing from Cyprus to Rome and to Paris and London without stopping in Cornwall; perhaps with a senior sergeant and some men stationed permanently in each city.

In the end, I only agreed about starting shipping services to London and Rome; I said I would have to think about having men permanently based in those cities and would want to talk to Thomas before I would agree.

I didn't explain why I was hesitant – because we want to keep our heads low so we don't attract attention from Richard or the members of his court; having a post in London might remind them of our existence. Rome, on the other hand might be a good place for a post since many of the refugees and pilgrims are Roman Catholics. Paris was definitely out – Richard might think we're supporting his Capetian enemy and Louis might think we're English spies.

Henry and Samuel Farmer spoke up next to report on the status of the apprentice archers we sent out last year. All but a few of them have learnt to walk together putting their feet down at the same time and are qualified as pike men and archers. The numbers were impressive.

All together including the new arrivals we now have almost thirteen hundred fully trained longbow-carrying archers home-based on Cyprus – men trained to fight on both land and sea! They are, of course, rarely present being as they are aboard our ships and permanently or temporarily based in other ports.

"And what about the apprentices we sent out last fall who didn't qualify?" Peter asked Samuel Farmer. *That's a good question, and I nodded my approval at Peter for asking it.*

"They're still rated as pike men and will be carrying pikes and swords until they qualify as archers. All in all, we've got about two hundred pike men still trying to qualify as archers and another couple of hundred or so who probably never will—they practise with their bows and their pikes and swords every day, of course, and would be useful inside the walls as defenders, but they spend most of their time working in our construction crews and smithy and suchlike.

"Both numbers are likely to go up, of course, after we evaluate and recruit from the slaves we just freed."

"How many slaves did we take out of Tunis?" I asked.

"At least a thousand and maybe more," said Harold. "I've got my sergeants sorting them out as we speak. Some of them are in very bad shape with the coughing pox. Mostly, they're sailors whose boats were taken or Christians the Moors captured in Spain. We've already found a number of Englishmen including a couple of archers who went out with that fool Sussex."

"Well, put those who need it on double and triple rations and make damn sure they have clothes and shelter—sometimes even the very slowest of them turn out to be sort of useful."

I said it with a great twinkle in my eyes and a nod towards Harold and Henry as everyone roared. *Well, that woke everyone up; Harold's a favourite of everyone, and Henry's a good man all around.*

Then we talked about many different things: the performance of our men stationed in Constantinople, Antioch, and Egypt—*no problems;* relations with the Templars and Hospitallers— *haven't heard from them* lately; the local governor and King Guy—*haven't heard from them either;* our stocks of arrows and bladed pikes—*large and growing;* and where best to use the new scribe Angelo del Gato— *probably right here in Cyprus.*

Finally, I called things to a halt; I was all talked out and I needed to take a break. *And so does everyone else from the looks of them. This heat is deadly.*

Chapter Seventeen

Everything Changes.

Things settled down rather quickly despite the sudden arrival of so many new men. The paying of the prize money went fairly smoothly and so did the aftermath—both because Henry and Harold forbid the carrying of weapons and because they had their steadiest sergeants patrolling the city's taverns and whorehouses carrying shields and swords.

Even more important, the local merchants prevailed upon the owners of Limassol's taverns and whorehouses to set up temporary tents outside the curtain wall under construction where the former slaves and refugee workers live in the shelters they have erected.

All of the city's taverns and whorehouses closed early on the day we paid out the prize money and the results were gratifying, if the rapes and fights are excluded — there were only three murders and we only had to hang a couple of recently released slaves for thieving. *And a surprising number of our own men deposited their prize coins in our chests and went on our parchment lists as people we owe deposited coins.*

The summer days that followed were hot despite the new Egyptian gowns. So hot, that Yoram temporarily reduced the length of the work and training day for most of our men to only ten hours and started it two hours before the sun arrived and began its daily trip around the world.

Everything changed three weeks later when a galley came in from Constantinople carrying an Orthodox priest. He's someone we know from Constantinople, Father Apostolos, and he was carrying a very surprising and disconcerting message for me — a ransom demand from the new Byzantium emperor in Constantinople, Alexios III.

Alexios's message was neither short nor sweet. He has taken Randolph and his men as prisoners and wanted us to pay a ransom of four thousand gold bezants to free them and their galleys. According to the Emperor's letter and

Father Apostolos, that's a fair price because the Emperor is entitled to all the property of everyone who helps his empire's traitors—and especially those who supported the previous Emperor he's just overthrown and replaced.

Randolph and his men, Alexios's letter stated, were paid to carry traitors from Constantinople to safety. As a result, the Emperor said he was going to keep our galleys and wanted four thousand gold bezants paid in ransom or Randolph and his men would be tortured and killed.

******

Father Apostolos merely shrugged when I ask him to explain the ransom demand and tell me what Randolph and his men did to deserve such a fate. His explanation, however, rang true.

"His Imperial Majesty needs money. He had to borrow many bezants from the church to buy off his brother's supporters so they would not interfere when he replaced his brother and took the throne for himself. Now he is looking everywhere for the coins he needs to repay us."

I immediately sent Father Apostolos back to the galley that brought him to Cyprus and sent runners to summon my lieutenants and senior sergeants. So far as I'm concerned the matter is settled—Randolph and Robert Monk and their men and galleys are either going to come back in one piece or a goodly number of Constantinople's gentry and priests are going into an early grave for me and my men to piss on.

I was in a rage and it's not good to act when you're upset. Even so, by the time the last of the men arrive all out of breath I'd studied my parchment map and had a response in mind. But first I wanted to take the temper of the men.

As soon as everyone was present, I read them the ransom note. Then I just stood there and looked at them without saying a word. To a man, they were as appalled and upset as I was, and their responses were exactly what I expected.

"Why, that rotten bastard."

"We're not going to abandon them, are we?"

"We've got to do something."

"Poor Randolph."

I finally spoke after everyone finished venting their anger.

"I've sent the messenger who delivered the ransom demand back to wait in the galley he arrived in. Some of us know him—he's the Patriarch's priest, the one we carried to Constantinople who arranged to have a galley standing by in Constantinople in case the Patriarch and his bishops would have to flee.

"I don't know whose side the priest's on or why he's carrying the ransom demand—but I'm going to find out and that's for damn sure. But, in a way, it doesn't matter because everybody needs to be clear about one thing. We are not going to abandon Randolph and his men no matter who ordered their capture or why."

I was quite distressed and determined when I leaned forward and laid down the law.

"We can't abandon any of our men no matter who they are or what it costs—it's in our contract; we made our marks, didn't we?"

Then I picked up the parchment I'd written and read out the response I had prepared whilst I was waiting for them to assemble—and watched as each of them grimly nodded his agreement.

"Due to a serious and most regrettable misunderstanding, some of your men are holding some of my men for ransom. The first ships and companies of men I am sending to Constantinople to free them will soon be in your waters and outside your walls. They will turn around and leave only if my men and galleys are returned unharmed—with an appropriate compensation for their hardships and the costs of our response. I also require quay space and a permanent concession to carry

people and cargos to and from Constantinople. If your prisoners are not freed with appropriate compensation, my men and I will immediately begin seizing your ships, burning your cities, and destroying your lands. William, Earl of Cornwall."

"I can send the message and I surely mean it. But if that's all we do at first I doubt the Emperor and his men will take our threats seriously. He'll not believe my response and may kill some or all our men to prove he will carry out his threat. It will also warn the Byzantines we'll be coming, though I doubt they'll believe it until they see our galleys.

"So I put it to you that my letter should not be sent until after we reach Constantinople with all of our galleys and men. After we take some of their galleys and transports, close their harbour, and prevent anyone from using their city gates, we can send the priest in with our message—because only then will the Emperor finally believe we're serious about not abandoning our men."

Everyone nodded and swore great curses and oaths. Then I swore the men who were present to absolute secrecy about our intention to attack Constantinople, and we began preparing lists of which of our galleys and men are to go and which are to stay and what each man is to do. It didn't take long.

Whilst we were making our lists, the sergeant captains of our galleys and cogs and other key personnel were hurriedly summoned to a meeting in the inner bailey. When they arrive, they'll be told we intend to make a big raid on Algiers which will sail in the next forty-eight hours and then stay there for at least thirty days to take the unsuspecting new arrivals coming into Algiers's harbour.

No one was told about our real destination or about the ransom demand until all the galleys and cogs going out in our initial fleet are anchored in the harbour and ready to sail. A good number of our recent prizes will remain behind so the rest can go out with a full company of fighting men on every galley.

******

Our meeting with the sergeant captains went well. In an effort to keep our actual destination a secret, I told the sergeants our raid on Tunis had been so successful we are going to leave in two days for Algiers and try to repeat it. The main difference being we intend to hold both the harbour and the land around the city walls for up to thirty days in order to take unsuspecting new arrivals as prizes as they enter the harbour.

The sergeants were enthusiastic about

another raid on the Moors to take more prizes. They listened carefully and nodded their heads in agreement when I told them to order their men not to mention to anyone that we would be going to Algiers.

Too many people will know about Algiers for the secret for it to be kept; word about a raid on Algiers should be all over the city within hours as our men head off to the taverns and whorehouses. Hopefully, if word of our preparations does get out, it will point everyone in the wrong direction.

******

It ended up taking three full days, but we were finally organised and the first of our galleys and fighting men were ready to leave for Constantinople.

We'd be sailing initially with about fifty galleys, six cargo cogs, and just over twelve hundred archers and four hundred trained and equipped pike men from among the apprentice archers. Harold will command the ships and Henry our land forces; Yoram and Joseph will stay behind here in Cyprus to insure we receive a steady flow of supplies and replacements. Peter will sail with me on Harold's galley as my assistant and the senior lieutenant.

Galleys and cogs returning from their regularly scheduled voyages to the Holy Land and elsewhere were to be immediately loaded with supplies and replacements and sent on to Constantinople to reinforce us.

******

Our basic plan was simple and easy to understand as good plans always are. We were going to go in with a surprise attack and try to either take all of Constantinople's galleys as prizes or destroy them. Then we were going to land our archers and pike men and lay a siege on the city until our men are released and our compensation is paid.

One look at the map and it was obvious that laying a siege on Constantinople would be easier said than done. It was little wonder sieges on the city have been tried many times and always failed.

Well, it will be interesting to see what the Greeks do when they find English archers snapping at their arses and coming at them from both land and sea. Besides, the goal of our attack and siege is not to fight our way into the city and conquer it as its previous besiegers were trying to do – our goal is only to hurt the Greeks and keep hurting them until they decide it would better to meet our relatively minor demands than keep fighting.

The great walled city of Constantinople is the capital city of the Byzantium Empire and receives most of its food and other supplies from the interior via the river that runs along its north wall and then into the Marmara Sea.

Accordingly, our biggest immediate challenge will be to get past the huge iron chain blocking the entrance to the river. Unless we can get some of our galleys past the chain, we won't be able to cut off the city's food and supplies coming in by water. Similarly, unless we bring a serious army ashore, we cannot cut the roads the Byzantines can use to bring in supplies by land.

Harold says the sailors call the river area inside the geat chain the Golden Horn; I wonder if it means there is gold there. I'll have to ask him.

If we can't get some of our galleys into the river and control its waters, the city will be able to get food as it is brought down the river or ferried over from the other shore. We obviously need to somehow get our galleys past the chain and be prepared in case we don't.

Even if we do get past the chain, controlling the sea and river waters, which are on three sides of the city, will not be enough. If we only control the water, the city will still be able to bring in food and reinforcements overland on the fourth side.

Once we get control of the waters around the city, and perhaps even if we cannot, we're going to spring a second surprise—we're going to land our men at the water supply closest to the north side of the city walls and cut off land access to the city as well.

Landing our archers and their supporting pike men will certainly surprise the city's defenders because we don't have many men compared to the number of people and soldiers in the city. They'll see our archers as not being a very strong force because we'll only have, at best, about twenty-three hundred fighting men plus the usual auxiliaries to carry water and such—and some of our fighting men will have to stay on our galleys to protect them even though we intend to destroy the Byzantine fleet before we send our archers ashore to fight on land.

There was nothing sure about how the Emperor will respond. But when he sees the relatively small size of our force, my lieutenants and I all think it likely the Byzantine army, such as it is, will come out of the city and fight in an effort to drive us away. We certainly hope so; they've never faced English archers using longbows and the long-handled pikes we've modified to add blades and hooks.

It's a good plan, but it will go nowhere and there will be problems if we don't take or destroy all of the Emperor's galleys on the Marmara Sea side of the iron chain. Control of the Marmara Sea is something we must have so they can't cut off our supply ships coming in from Cyprus. *Or our withdrawal route if we have to run for it.*

Failing to immediately seize or destroy all their galleys would be a big and, perhaps, fatal problem. Harold says it's quite possible the Byzantine galleys we don't take in our initial surprise attack will come against us with two weapons we haven't faced before—long, pointed rams sticking out in front of their bows and some kind of fire-throwing device the Emperor's navy uses to burn up enemy ships.

According to Harold, it's called "Greek Fire" and no one knows exactly what it is or how it is made and delivered—only that it will be very dangerous if we let one of Constantinople's galleys get close enough to use it against one of our galleys.

Our best answer to the problem, of course, is to quickly destroy their galleys so they can't begin using their secret weapon against us. Accordingly, attempting to destroy the Byzantine fleet with a surprise attack is exactly what we are going to try to do.

It's a strange problem, isn't it? On the sea, we will have the numbers and they will have the latest weapons; on the land, they will have numbers and we will have the latest weapons.

One thing is certain. We're not taking any chances about word of our destination leaking out to warn the Emperor's men we're coming. The priest is coming with us and won't be unchained from the rowing deck of Harold's galley until we're away from shore. Similarly, our men will initially be told that our destination is Algiers so we can take more prizes.

A raid on Algiers makes sense after our success at Tunis. The men will believe it and undoubtedly talk about it in the local taverns and whorehouses – which is exactly what we want.

Our men won't learn of our real destination until after we are out of the harbour and on our way Constantinople.

Chapter Eighteen
The Byzantine fleet.

It took longer than we thought to get ready. It wasn't until three days later that we sailed out of the Limassol with about sixty fighting men on each of our forty-nine galleys and a lot of volunteer rowers and auxiliaries from among the refugees and the freed slaves and, to my surprise, the local fishermen. Until a few minutes after we rowed out of the harbour, everyone thought they were going to Algiers for more prizes.

Our men didn't learn the truth and why it was kept from them until the day we sailed. Only in the morning, when every galley was anchored in the harbour and ready to sail, did we tell them—when Harold issued a call for the sergeant captains of each galley to report to his galley to get their sailing orders.

The sergeant captains were shocked and just as distressed and furious when they heard about our men and galleys being held for ransom as my lieutenants and I had been when we first heard about it. They were visibly pleased and excited when they heard what we intend to do to get them back, starting with either taking the entire Byzantine fleet as prizes or destroying it.

"And one last message for every one of you to remind his men—our contract clearly states that no man will ever be abandoned; it's important every man know, in the name of God, we truly mean it when we promise never to desert our men; and that's why we are going to Constantinople for our prizes and prize money instead of Algiers."

As soon as the meeting ended, the grim-faced and excited sergeant captains hurried to their dinghies and rowed back to their galleys. They immediately raised their anchors and headed out to sea. Only after they cleared the harbour would they explain the situation to their men.

We sailed with many volunteers to help with the rowing and other chores. We have them because two days ago we announced a guarantee of prize money of at least twenty silver coins to every man who goes with us. It got a good response because twenty silver coins is more than most of the freed slaves and fishermen could expect to earn in the rest of their lifetimes. *It also helped when Yoram announced all able-bodied workers and former slaves who don't go with us will no longer be fed or employed.*

******

Our galleys and cogs were jammed with men and piled high with food and supplies as we headed northwest towards the Aegean Sea and on into the Dardanelles, the long narrow waterway leading into the Marmara Sea and Constantinople. *And many of our galleys were quickly modified before we left Limassol to enlarge their rope-enclosed lookout nests so they could hold as many as four archers to shoot down on enemy decks.*

The Dardanelles was the logical place for the Emperor's navy to try to intercept us if they know we're coming. It's a busy waterway and quite long and narrow. It would be hard for us to get away from their hull-puncturing rams and Greek Fire if they knew we are coming and were determined to ram or burn us. But we had no choice—we had to pass through the narrow Dardanelle straits to get to Constantinople. It was the first of the city's many natural defences.

******

Henry and I stood next to Harold and watched as he led our strongest and fastest five galleys through the waterway. It took most of the day, and we saw many cargo transports both coming and going—but we didn't see a single Byzantine galley until we came out the other end of the narrow passage and rowed into the Marmara Sea.

The cargo transports paid us no mind and we didn't bother them; they seemed to think they were protected by having paid their tolls and being in Byzantine waters. Once we hailed a single-masted Arab dhow and came alongside of it to ask if there are any Byzantine war galleys waiting near the exit. None, they said, except for the usual two toll collectors—and then looked at us in surprise when they realised the implications of the question.

And that's exactly what we found as we come out of the Dardanelles and entered the Marmara Sea—two, side-by-side Byzantine galleys. They appeared to be watching the passing ships to make sure they've paid their required tolls and bribes. Most of the passing ships were known to them and didn't stop.

The presence of the two galleys was not a

surprise, our sergeant captains had seen them before—this was where one or two Byzantine galleys were usually stationed to collect tolls and bribes. The Arab dhow had merely confirmed what we already knew—and, much more importantly, told us the Byzantine fleet was not waiting for us.

Our galleys were not known to the Byzantines, of course, so it was no surprise when some of the oars on the lower rowing deck of the closest of the two toll-collecting galleys finally started to move and it turned to come towards us. It was similarly no surprise to them when our galleys turned leisurely toward them.

Our behaviour of coming to them was viewed by the Byzantines as quite normal because it was expected—the Byzantine Empire controls both the Sea of Marmara on this side of the city and the Black Sea and the Bosphorus waterway leading to it on the other side. The empire's galley crews were familiar with the deference paid to them by other sailing vessels.

Normality reigned until at the last second when someone on the Byzantine galley finally realised we didn't intend to peacefully come to a stop and let them board to collect the usual bribes and fees. By then, we were almost on top of them and it was far too late for the Byzantines to have any hope of getting away.

Harold suddenly shouted the order for our oars to be pulled in and seconds later our hull began shearing off some of the Byzantine's oars as we threw our grapples and the archers in the lookout's nest and on our deck began shooting. Almost at the same time, one of our sister galleys was similarly launching arrows and breaking off some of the unsuspecting Byzantine's oars on the other side.

Within seconds our victim's deck was covered with dead and wounded men, and boarders from both of our galleys were pouring on to her deck virtually unopposed. The other Byzantine galley tried to get away but soon met the same fate at the hands of the other three galleys in our vanguard.

"We caught them totally by surprise," Harold commented a few minutes later as he and Henry and I were walking around our prize's deck and commenting on how unprepared it was to fight.

"What's really encouraging is how few sailors and fighting men they have on board. There are only slaves on the lower rowing benches to row and a few men to steer and collect the bribes and taxes. On the other hand, it sure as hell has a ram just under the surface of the water. Come up to the bow and take a look."

And it certainly did; looking down at the water from where we were standing at the front of our prize, we could see a long sinister shadow a few feet under the surface. It protruded twenty feet or more from the front of our prize. Our galleys don't have such rams—this would be a dangerous war galley in the hands of a proper crew and there is no question about it.

"Whoa, that thing hits a ship's hull and it's going to punch a big hole; sink it, for sure," I said.

"You're right about that," Harold agreed. "That's the bad thing; the good thing is there is nothing on board that looks like it could start a fire. I wonder if the stories about the empire's 'Greek Fire' are lies similar to those we told about going off to raid another Moorish port?"

A few minutes later, we pulled alongside the other Byzantine galley and got very much the same report. There weren't very many sailors and fighting men on this one either.

We left small prize crews behind to chain the surviving Byzantines to their own rowing benches, inform their slaves they'd unchained and freed when they reached Cyprus, and tend to the wounded. Both of the prizes will join the main column of our galley and cogs, which is now pouring out of the Dardanelles waterway behind us.

Harold is elated. He thinks the sight of two quick prizes will greatly encourage the men; let's hope the rest of the Byzantine navy is equally unprepared.

Five minutes later, we were back on board our galley and the ships in our armada had at least one man on every oar. We'd be spending the rest of the day and coming night rowing hard for the quays and wharves around Constantinople where the Byzantine galleys are usually tied up.

****** *William*

Uncertainty as to the size of the Byzantine fleet and how prepared it would be to fight had dominated our discussions before we left Cyprus. Estimates we'd heard from our sergeant captains and sailors who've been here previously ranged all over the place. All we knew for sure was that we were going up against the galleys and fighting men of the world's greatest empire.

The consensus of the sergeant captains and veteran sailors was that the Byzantines had about forty poorly maintained and under-manned galleys, and that they mostly stay in the waters around Constantinople. Apparently, those galleys, and a few in the relatively small Black Sea, are all the Byzantines need to collect the tolls and keep the Moorish and other pirates away from the city.

Constantinople came into sight several hours after the sun rose and began passing overhead the next morning. From the roof of our galley's stern castle, an hour later, we could see what looked to be about thirty galleys as we approached the wooden wharf and the nearby beach where the Byzantine navy's galleys were moored and beached. Most of them were nosed into the beach.

Thirty sounded about right. We've been told they usually keep another ten to twelve galleys in the Black Sea, which is surrounded by the various subject kingdoms and principalities of the empire. And, of course, they have several of our galleys as well, the ones which probably came in fat, dumb, and happy to unload refugees. They were captured after they tied up at one of the city's many quays to unload their passengers.

Harold hoisted his "follow me" and "engage" flags and our entire armada went straight for the galleys in front of us like foxes when they see a chicken. Every one of our galleys was rowing hard to be the first to board one of the Byzantine galleys and take it as a prize—except for the five galleys which will row right past them and continue on around the city walls to see if they can get past the great chain and into the river.

"Remember, lads," Harold shouted first on

the main deck and then on the lower rowing deck, "some of those galleys are probably ours and some of our men are likely to be chained to the rowing benches. Go easy on who you kill."

It was a warning the sergeant captains of every one of our galleys had been ordered to repeat to their men before they began their attack. Harold and I both made it clear that I would go very hard on any sergeant if one of our captured men dies and he didn't remind his men about the possibility some of our archers might be on the rowing benches of the galleys he and his men were trying to take as prizes.

******

We fell upon the beached and moored Byzantine galleys and the men standing around them like a pack of hungry wolves upon a flock of sleeping sheep. There was no other way to describe it. Our surprise was total and our men had their blood up and were spoiling for a fight—because they were attacking in an attempt to rescue our fellow archers in addition to the promised prize money.

The Byzantines didn't have a chance. There were very few sailors on board their galleys, and they were quickly cut down despite their desperate pleas for mercy. So were those who had been standing on the quay and beach and didn't have the wit to run away before it was too late.

"English? Are there English here?" That was the cry I heard repeated over and over again as our men poured on to the Byzantine galleys along the beach and rushed down to the slaves on their lower rowing decks with barely a pause to cut down their luckless crews.

Harold and Peter and I first heard the calls coming across the water to where Harold has us nosed into the beach next to one of the Byzantine galleys. Moments later, it began in the galley next to us even as some of Harold's men were still splashing ashore to board it and push it out into the water as a prize.

******

Less than twenty minutes later and it was all over. We've recaptured our two missing galleys and taken twenty-nine of theirs as prizes. More importantly, we'd freed Randolph and a number of his men. They'd been chained to the rowing benches of their own galleys. Robert Monk, one of our galleys, and some of Randolph's men were still missing. They'd been taken away and Randolph and his men had not seen them since.

According to our men who knew the Byzantines,

prisoners and criminals taken by the Byzantines have only two fates – they either have their heads immediately chopped off or they are sent to die slowly as galley slaves. We can only hope that Robert and the other men are on the missing galley.

Several times during our attack, armed men came out of the city gate and started towards the beach where we were milling around the various galleys. The first were a handful of men, probably gate guards, who came running out to see what the commotion is all about and why screaming and shouting people were running into the city from the beach and quay.

Our men had fairly much followed their instructions and let the unarmed men running for the city walls escape. The gate guards coming towards them carrying arms were another story – the first five or six didn't get very far before they almost all went down in a sudden shower of arrows from our nearest archers.

From where I'm standing on Harold's deck, it looked like all of our archers on our galley nearest to the gate began loosing at the same time and stopped at the same time; probably when their sergeant gave the word.

About ten minutes later, a much larger group of armed men came running out of the same city gate, perhaps thirty men in all. They met the same fate from an even greater storm of arrows; although, a few were able to turn back in time to get inside the city before the gate was shut.

The ground in front of the gate nearest the Byzantine fleet's wharf and beach was littered with dead and wounded men, and faces were beginning to appear on the high city wall when something unexpected happens—several of our men jogged up to the wall and begin nonchalantly picking up the arrows lying about and jerking them out of the men on the ground.

I watch as they both suddenly stop at the same time and ran back. A sergeant must have shouted an order. *I wonder if he sent them; it suddenly made me wonder if we've brought enough arrows?*

And look who's here, by God.

"Hello, Randolph, old friend; it's good to see your ugly face."

"It's good to see your ugly face too, William, by God. Thankee for coming for me and the lads. Thankee, indeed. I knowed you'd come; that's what I've been telling the lads ever since they catched us. Took us by surprise, didn't they? The bastards. It were the priest what done for us."

"Say that again. What priest?"

******

Randolph told us his tale as we stood on the deck of Harold's galley and watched our galleys and their prizes come off the beach.

"It's true, I tell you. It's true. They planned it all along, the priests and the new Emperor. Wanted their enemies to show themselves, didn't they? And they wanted our galleys and coins too; damn their eyes. The bastard laughed when he told me how they'd gulled us, didn't he? Proud of himself, he was—and angry as a wet hen because you helped the old Emperor get away with their coins."

"Are you talking about the priest we boarded at Antioch who brought all the coins and custom to us here in Constantinople?"

"Aye, that's the one."

"Well then, old friend, I've a big surprise for you."

Chapter Nineteen

Our galleys travel overland.

Our galleys scattered to their various individual assignments as soon as they finished with their part of the assault on the Byzantine navy. Some headed up the Bosphorus channel to stop any shipping from coming to Constantinople from the Black Sea and a couple of others headed back to block the Dardanelles and take prizes from among those coming through the strait to enter the Marmara.

Unfortunately, not everything went so well — none of our galleys assigned to move into the river on the north side of the city were able to do so. A great chain blocked their way.

Most of our galleys, those carrying the great mass of our archers and pike men, rowed around the city wall until they came to where a little stream ran into the ocean. That's where we nosed into the beach and began to unload our fighting men and their supplies and auxiliaries. We were about three miles from the outer wall on the land side of the city.

****** *William*

"Don't forget to put a line of our volunteers as sentries along the stream; we don't want any man or animal to piss or shite anywhere near where we'll dip out the water we drink," I reminded Henry before I went back down to the lower rowing bench to get more information from Father Apostolos. "We'll never hear the end of it from Thomas if we don't."

My brother Thomas is keen about such things because the book he read at monastery said that's what the Romans did. I know he'll ask about our camp and be angry if we didn't do it. It can't hurt, can it?

Randolph and I had a chance to talk to Father Apostolos whilst we're rowing over to where our army will land. He had some quite funny ideas, probably because he was both a Greek and a priest.

At first, he wouldn't talk to us because he had somehow gotten it into his head we wouldn't hurt him because he was a priest and doing so would cause us to burn in hell. His attitude changed when I promptly cut off one of his fingers and told him I'd be cutting off his balls next and then his dingle. After he stopped screaming, he told us everything.

"We thought you'd pay to get your men and galleys back; it wasn't because you are Latins, it was because we needed the coins," he sobbed as I patted him on the back and nodded my understanding.

Latins, of course, as I explained to Harold who came down to see what all the noise and fuss was about, is what the Byzantines call everyone who looks to Rome for their religion — because *Rome's priests speak to each other and pray at their faithful in Latin.*

What we learnt from Father Apostolos was quite interesting. Randolph was right — it was all a plot of the new Emperor and his advisors to get the deposed Emperor's supporters to identify themselves so they could be eliminated.

Apparently, the new Emperor borrowed heavily from the Church and from the Venetian moneylenders so he could bribe the Byzantine military and other members of the royal family to abandon his brother, the former Emperor, so he could become the Emperor in his place. It worked.

The idea was that the Church would be repaid with the money the old Emperor's supporters paid to escape, and the Venetians, by the sale or ownership of our galleys and the granting of more trade concessions. That's why they arranged for so many of our galleys to be hired.

It worked up to a point—they took our galleys and arrested and killed some of the old Emperor's courtiers as they came to the galleys to make their escape. In effect, everything went off as planned and Alexios became emperor except we somehow got away with the refugee coins that were supposed to be used to repay the Church and the Venetians.

The priest claimed it was the Venetians' idea to get the refugee coins back by holding our men and galleys for ransom. They knew our company used one of the standard crusader contracts pledging no man would be left behind. They rightly thought we would honour it if we could. That's why getting the refugee coins back as a ransom was their backup plan if we got away with them.

What did not even enter the minds of the Emperor's advisors, according to Father Apostolos, was the possibility we might attack Constantinople to retrieve our men instead of paying the ransom—they could not conceive of it being possible for a handful of Latins from England to successfully attack the great Byzantine Empire and hold it to ransom instead of the other way around.

******

It was still cool in the early morning. Our men had spent most of the night unloading our equipment and supplies and erecting the tents we brought with us so they'd have some shade during the hot summer days. Now they were sleeping in their battle ranks with their pikes and swords and bows by their sides.

It's no wonder the men were able to sleep — most of them had been awake for two straight days and some even longer.

Of course, we knew enough to bring our linen shade tents with us; we've been in Cyprus for a couple of years, where it gets even hotter in the summer than it does here.

Henry and I were still awake, and Harold had just come ashore and joined us. Father Apostolos was still moaning about his missing finger and pretending to sleep in the galley beached immediately behind us. I brought Harold up to date on what we'd learnt.

"What we've learnt from the priest explains a lot. But it doesn't change the reality that we're here with a small and outnumbered force of men and the city can still get food and provisions both by land

and by sea. We've got to change that reality. So here's what we're going to do tonight after the sun goes down."

We were still looking at the map and talking about the details when one of our sentries gave a great warning shout. The city gate closest to us was opening. Moments later, a small party of horsemen rode out and headed straight for our camp.

"Bring me the leather message quiver from the forecastle," I ordered one of the archers standing nearby. Then I picked up my bow, clapped my straw sun hat on my head, motioned for my little squad of personal guards to follow me, and walked out to meet the horsemen. Harold and Henry stayed behind.

There were four of them and ten of us.

A rather arrogant-looking fellow with fancy clothes and a great huge turban on his head was their leader. He pulled his horse to a stop about ten feet in front of us. I interrupted him when he started to say something in Greek.

"Latin, French, or English," I said in Latin with a dismissive shake of my hand as my runner jogged up and handed me the leather message case with my response to the ransom demand.

"The general doesn't speak Latin. He wants to speak to your leader," one of the riders offered in bad French.

"He'll have to make do with me. But I'm rather sure this is what he wants." That's what I said in French as I handed the leather pouch back to my messenger and motioned for him to take it to the man who seemed to be in charge.

"There are two parchments inside," I said. "One is your ransom demand. The other is our response. They will tell you all you need to know. Our demands are quite reasonable under the circumstances—we will leave when you deliver the rest of our men you are holding for ransom and ten thousand gold bezants. I suggest you move promptly. The price for saving your lives and your city will be one thousand gold bezants higher tomorrow and increase again by that much every day thereafter."

The Byzantine riders appear dumbfounded by me, their reception, and my response. Ten minutes later I was back under the shade of my tent and they were trotting through the distant city gate. It was getting seriously hot.

******

That very evening, as soon as the sun finished passing overhead, our somewhat rested men hauled one of our smaller and sturdier galleys out of the water on log rollers and began moving it across the peninsula of land to the water on the other side. We followed the dirt path that ran along the little stream and brought our weapons and our bales of arrows with us.

The area outside the city walls was surprisingly empty of buildings and villages. It was farmland and pasture; those who work it must live in the city. The only living things near us were some cattle and a couple of horses—they'll be roasting over our cooking fires when we stop to eat in the morning.

Not surprising us at all was that there was no one about for us to question. They farmworkers must have run when we arrived. In the distance we could see quite a bit of movement coming in and out of the city. There must be a road up ahead.

All night long we pulled on the long tow lines and the galley slowly moved forward. Teams of men picked up the rounded logs as it passed over them and ran them around to put them in front of the galley again. When the sun came up, the galley was almost two miles inland and our shade tents were up. Everyone was openly wagering on how soon the Byzantines would launch an attack.

Henry and I were kneeling down by a parchment map and most of the men were sleeping, when who should walk up but Harold with a group of armed sailors. It was a couple of hours after sunrise. I recognised some of his men as being from the crew of his personal galley and nodded to them with a smile of recognition.

They're from Harold's galley crew and clearly very curious about what we were doing. Harold waved his unspoken approval and they soon wandered off to marvel at the galley being moved on land.

Harold was the bearer of good news.

"The waters hereabouts are clear of Byzantine galleys, and we've got the waterways blocked so no ships can get to the city. The only warships from the Bosphorus to the Mediterranean are five Venetian galleys beached across the way at the Venetian concession."

"Good. Does that mean you can free up some of the archers and rowers who are still on your galleys?"

"Aye, it does. But there's something else; two of the prizes have some something strange on board. They've each got a great huge smith's leather bellows to pump air. It's attached to a big iron kettle full of liquid that smells funny, and there's a long iron bar with a hole in the middle attached to the kettle. I think it's the fire thing we've been hearing about, the Greek Fire thing."

"Interesting. Hmm. Well, send them straight back to Cyprus with prize crews. Tell Yoram to keep them safe until we have a chance to find out how they work. Do the slaves know?"

"They had no slaves aboard them, neither galley."

"Well, maybe some of the other slaves or we can take some prisoners who know how the thing works. Did you free the slaves yet?"

"That's one of the things I've come to talk to you about. I know how you feel about freeing serfs and slaves. But most of these don't look like honest sailor men what got captured with their ships.

"I think they're mostly felons and murderers who've been sent off to die slowly instead of being topped for a quick death. I've got a sailor man who speaks the Greek on William Smith's galley. I'm going to send him around with a couple of sergeants to free any English and Norman slaves, but if it's all right with you I'll feed the rest real good but keep them in chains until we can sort them out."

"Aye, that's probably best. But be sure to move the men you free to other galleys."

"Of course; I'm not daft, am I?"

"Only when it comes to women and the best ale to drink," was Henry's teasing response.

We might have stood there and bantered for a few moments except all around us the men who have been resting suddenly begin standing up and pointing and talking loudly — the landward city gate was open and an army was coming out.

"Best you and your sailors get back to your galley whilst there's still time."

Chapter Twenty

Constantinople's army attacks.

Our camp of shade tents was organised into a square next to the galley we are moving along the little stream. The companies in each of our four battle groups were camped facing in a different direction with our supplies and non-fighting auxiliaries in the middle of the square. It made us instantly organised to fight off an attack no matter from which direction it might come. *Thomas says it's how the old Romans did their camping. It makes sense; yes, it does.*

Henry and I immediately climbed the little wooden ladders the sailors made to let us see over the tops of our men's tents and heads. There were three ladders; a squad of pike men made sure they followed the square wherever it went. They reached up about as high as a tall man might stretch his hand.

What what Henry and I watched when we

climbed the ladders was rather encouraging. The Byzantines were being led out into the hot and sunny open area between us and the city walls by four or five hundred horsemen, undoubtedly their knights and mounted men-at-arms. Behind them came thousands and thousands of men walking in what appears to be a disorganised mass.

Off to the side of the Byzantine army a smaller party of mounted men clustered together next to a brightly coloured tent that went up as we watched — the King and his courtiers had come out to watch their army massacre the little band of foolish invaders.

******

Once again a small group of horsemen moved forward.

"They want to talk," Henry offered unnecessarily.

"That's fine. I'm willing to talk, not that I think it will do any good. But you never know, do you? Wait here. I'll be right back."

And with that, I climbed down from my ladder and walked through the ranks of the battle group facing the growing mass of Byzantines in the distance. My little group of guards walked along behind me.

Peter's battle group faced the growing horde of Byzantines. He was standing immediately in front of his men waiting for me.

"Are we ready?" I asked him. I already know the answer because I've just been looking down at his men and walked through them. But I want to give him a chance to say something for his men.

"Oh, I should think so. We've got way more than enough arrows and pikes to take care of that lot."

"That's what it looks like to me too. They remind me of a herd of sheep walking towards a pack of wolves." *I answered rather loudly so the men around me could here. It was a good description to spread through the ranks and I'm sure it will.*

Then I walked about thirty paces in front of our men and stopped with my guards in a half moon immediately behind me. I was wearing my chain mail under my white cotton gown and there were seven black stripes on its front and back. The sergeant of my guards had three stripes, his chosen man two, and each of the others have one—every man was an experienced archer.

"I suspect they'll be a bit of treachery to put some fear into us," I said to my guards softly under my breath. "But don't push an arrow at anyone unless he pulls his sword; kill anyone who does."

The Greeks are famous for their treachery, aren't they? At least, that's what the Church says. And it must be true since they're constantly killing their leaders and replacing them.

"That's far enough," I said in French as I held up my hand. There were six of them this time including the one from yesterday who speaks French. This time several of them actually look like they might be serious fighting men instead of courtiers wearing huge turbans to prove they are important.

One of them had a particularly intense look on his face and was holding his unsheathed sword next to his horse's neck.

"Are you here to bring me my men and coins, or are you here to die?" I inquired in French with a sweet tone to my voice. *To die, for sure.*

Before the man can answer, I turned to my guards and in a conversational tone gave an order in English to the sergeant and his chosen man.

"Willy, Rufe, point a shaft at the man on the left with his sword in his hand. Push one into him quickly if he starts to use it. You too, Robert. The rest of you watch the others—but only launch at those who actually raise a blade to attack us."

"The Emperor commands you to leave

immediately. If you do not, we will slaughter you all without mercy."

"How strange. That is exactly the message I have for you. Take your sad excuse for an army back inside the city before it is too late for you. But I do have a question for you."

"A question?"

"Yes, a question. Is it true what your soldiers say about the big, funny-looking turbans you wear being used to identify the nobles who are too cowardly to fight?" *I'm provoking them, aren't I? I hope so.*

The translation of my insult got an immediate response from the arrogant young man holding the sword. He dug his heels into his horse and started to raise his sword. His effort was only partially successful—the horse came at me and he didn't; he was knocked backwards off the horse by three arrows that went through his chain mail and into his chest up to their fletchings.

"Nice horse," I said as I grabbed its bridle when it bolted towards me as its rider slid out of the saddle. "I'll keep it as a remembrance." Then I turned around and walked back to our square leading my new horse. *I've never had a horse of my own before. It's all black.*

My visitors hauled their horses around and

galloped back to the tent by the distant wall. *I wonder if the Emperor and his courtiers are there to watch. I hope so.*

******

My new horse had been hobbled, and I was back on my ladder talking to Henry who was standing on his when the Byzantine army finally started moving forward. It looked like a mob of looters led by a bunch of fox hunters on horses. They were a couple of miles away and were coming straight at us.

There wasn't much chance of such a mob being able to change direction and hit us in the flanks or from behind. The fools were coming straight at us. Bad luck for them.

Most of our men were still under the tents but ready to instantly move out of them and into the hot sunlight.

"Battle Groups Straighten Line with Flank Protection Three," I heard Henry say to the sergeant who has climbed to the very top of the third ladder—who promptly repeated the order in each direction with the clearest and loudest voice I'd ever heard.

"Good, isn't he," Henry asked me with a smile as he nodded towards the archer sergeant with the very big voice. Instantly, we could hear the order being repeated by the sergeants all around us. Within moments our square began spreading out into a battle line with pike men in the first three ranks, archers in the next five ranks after a gap of ten paces, and two or three water carriers and other auxiliaries behind them—and instantly each company's auxiliaries scurried to move the tents to once again shade their men.

Our archers could all launch their arrows from our square, but this formation will give our archers the best look at the approaching army and thus the most accuracy. It's little wonder our companies of archers and pike men move into it so smoothly—Henry and his sergeants have them practise walking back and forth from battle squares to battle lines as part of every training day. The only addition for today was the use of each company's auxiliaries to move its tents.

"String bows. Stand by with longs."

"Pike men, prepare to set butts. Pike men, kneel."

******

It took the straggling mob that passed for the Byzantine army the better part of half an hour to cross the two miles or so from the city wall and then stop about two hundred yards in front of our front line. Even those in the rear of the mob were well within range of our archers, although, they almost certainly did not yet know it. Their horsemen were grouped in the centre. There looked to be about five hundred horses and as many as twenty thousand men on foot.

"Flank Protection Two; first line switch to heavies. Flank Protection Two; first line switch to heavies."

"Good call, Henry. What do you think? Should we keep waiting?"

What we were doing was waiting until they started to surge forward to begin their attack. When they surge is when their commanders will lose control and be unable to order a retreat.

Henry didn't have a chance to answer. Suddenly, the flags around the horsemen begin to be waved in big circles and the Byzantine army began to move forward with many great cheers and shouts. It instantly raised a great cloud of dust.

Their horsemen began walking their horse towards us with the men walking and running in a great huge mass behind them. The feet of the horses and the walking men were kicking up clouds of dust. It was time to learn them about the range of longbows.

"PUSH CONTINUOUS! DON'T STOP!,"

Henry shouted and his loud talker began repeating over and over again.

The sky was suddenly filled with a continuous cloud of well-aimed arrows — and they all began coming down on the poor sods riding and running towards us. Horses fell, and the mob became like a baited animal that suddenly begins writhing and trembling as darts and stabs pour on to it from all sides.

******

All around me I heard the grunts as our archers pushed out their bows to give the shots more power and distance. Almost immediately, the unarmoured men running in the cloud of dust behind the sword-waving horsemen began to slow down and turn around as more and more of them went down.

What was left of the horsemen keep coming — they dropped their helmet visors, broke into a gallop, and were waving their swords over their heads as they closed on us. Some of their foot were still running towards us but were falling further and further behind the horsemen.

For the first time arrows were beginning to fall in our ranks and our men are beginning to go down, but only a few. Some of the Byzantine archers were obviously still functioning in the mob of men milling around in the huge cloud of dust in front us; they had gotten close enough for their short bows to become effective.

It was hard to pick out their archers because there was a great huge dust cloud in front of us and it was getting bigger and bigger and slowly drifting towards us.

One of my guards handed a ship's shield up to me and I instinctively raise it just in time for an arrow to slam into it. Henry already had his shield up. That's when I finally realised that standing on ladders so we can see was making us juicy targets for the Byzantine archers in the huge cloud of dust rising in front of us.

"Raise your pikes. Raise your pikes." I heard Henry boom out through his talker as another arrow thudded into my shield.

A few seconds later, what was left of the Byzantine horsemen begin to reach us and crash into our lines.

We should have put out stakes and caltrops. That's what I was thinking as I watched the first of the galloping horses crash into our front lines and impale themselves on our pikes. The horses had no armour.

Some of the horsemen saw the pikes held by our kneeling pike men come up in time to turn aside but most didn't. And in their final moments of life, they cause us serious damage and confusion — because so many of them flew off their impaled and suddenly stopped horses and into our ranks.

For a brief moment, there was a reduction in the volume of arrows we were delivering. But it quickly ended as the archers who had been knocked down by the unhorsed riders tumbling into our ranks picked themselves up and resumed pushing out arrows.

I didn't see it happen. One of the unhorsed riders tumbled through the ranks of our men and knocked my ladder over. I came down hard on top of the fallen ladder and, for a few seconds, all I knew was that I was on the ground holding my bow with one hand and a shield with the other.

Numerous hands pulled me to my feet and helped steady me as I climbed back up the first few steps of Henry's ladder in an effort to see what was happening. The ladder with the loud sergeant was also on the ground in pieces or I'd have taken that one.

What I saw was alarming. A few of the Byzantine horsemen had survived and were riding off, but those who flew off their horses and smashed into our men had caused gaps and disruptions in our lines.

Various things happen simultaneously as I got back on my feet and climb a couple of steps up Henry's ladder—our sergeants and men were scrambling to their feet and closing ranks to fill the gaps; our delivery of arrows diminished as some of the archers begin to run out and the sergeants stopped shooting whilst they pushed the men into place to fill the line; and the dust cloud full of the Byzantine foot reached our lines and began going past us on both the left and the right.

Only a few of the Byzantine foot reach our lines looking to fight. Most of those who reached us appeared to be stunned and confused by the incredible noise and surprised to find themselves face to face with our men in the cloud of dust.

I could clearly see many them trying to back away when they realised they'd reached our lines. And those who still wanted to fight were being hampered by having to walk around the dead and struggling men and horses all along our front in order to reach our front line.

Those of the Byzantine foot who are still willing to fight were also being hampered by being totally hot and exhausted as a result of their long walk in the hot sun. Our men, by contrast, were well watered and had spent most of the day resting in the shade.

Most of the overheated and exhausted Byzantine foot appeared to be barely trained and poorly armed militia. Our pike men, on the other hand, may not have yet earned the right to wear the stripe of a qualified archer, but every one of them had spent part of each day practising with a sword and shield and pike. And right behind them were the best archers in the world who, in self-defence, were lowering their aims to take out the Byzantine foot immediately in front of them.

The result was a slaughter with a virtual wall of dead and dying Byzantine foot and horsemen piling up all along our front lines as the great cloud of dust they've raised slowly drifted in to engulf us all. And somehow I badly needed to piss. So I lifted my gown and pissed even though I was still standing below Henry on his ladder. It certainly was dusty and hot.

******

The withdrawal of the Byzantine army quickly turned into a panic-stricken rout with desperate men throwing away their weapons and running for their lives towards the city gate they had bravely exited earlier this morning. And once they started running, they were right to throw their weapons away and run as fast as possible—because Henry ordered a counter-attack and they were indeed running for their lives.

"Archers, stand firm and loose; Pike men, charge. Pike men, charge."

"That's it; chase them, lads; kill them if they don't surrender."

******

An hour or so later, Henry and I walked through the battlefield towards the distant city gate. It was incredibly hot, and all around us our men were picking up weapons and giving a soldier's mercy to the wounded Byzantines who needed one and some who didn't.

Henry blamed himself for not killing more of them.

"I held the archers back under the shade tents because of the enemy foot who got around us on our flanks in the confusion. Otherwise, we'd have gotten even more of them."

"You don't have to apologise for not killing more of them, my friend. It was a good decision and a great victory. The men you trained did very well, very well indeed. Now let's go make sure our wounded are being tended to and get something to drink whilst we wait to hear from the Emperor."

We waited all day and heard not a word from the city. The next morning the city gate opened and a procession of priests walks out of the main gate carrying little handheld tents on sticks to keep the sun off their heads. Two of the Emperor's courtiers were with them.

I did not go out of my tent to meet them and I did not offer them a place to sit in the shade or a drink when they finally reached the shade tent where Randolph, Henry, Peter, and I were sitting.

"Now what do you propose?" I asked the head courtier rather benignly in French as I stood up and walked to the edge of the shade so they'd be in the sun.

"The Emperor has graciously agreed that there is a misunderstanding and that you are entitled to the ten thousand gold coins to compensate you for your trouble."

"Surely, you either jest or take me as a fool? You just attacked us," I said to him rather angrily as I leaned forward and poked him in the shoulder for emphasis. He was taken aback by my behaviour. *People don't do that to you, do they?*

"I told you it was ten thousand bezants and all the rest of my missing men and galleys and only if they all were immediately freed. You refused my offer and attacked us instead.

"Now the price to save your city and Emperor from burning is twenty-five thousand gold bezants and ten thousand more if you don't immediately produce my missing men and galleys. I'll take the equivalent in silver if you don't have enough gold.

"I also want all Latin slaves within your empire immediately freed, permanent mooring space for at least three cogs and galleys that is acceptable to me, an acceptable compound near a city gate for use as a shipping post, and the right to carry passengers and cargo to and from Constantinople without fees or taxes."

"But that's impossible."

"You're wrong. It's quite possible and you know it."

"His Imperial Highness will never agree."

"Those are my minimum requirements, and my offer is only good for one day. Either you provide my men and the coins by tomorrow morning or we will continue with our preparations to sack the city and kill the Emperor. And since we do not trust you, we are going to proceed as if you will not pay. Accordingly, tonight when it is cooler we'll be bringing more galleys across to the river and proceed with our plan to starve you out and sack the city."

And that's exactly what we did. The second and third galleys were easier to move, and by sunup observers on the city wall could see three of our galleys well inland and on their way to block the river.

Several hours later, the courtiers came once again. This time there are no priests among them.

"The Emperor has agreed to all of your requests for the damage caused by his people. The city's merchants and the Church will pay the thirty-five thousand bezants." *They'll pay thirty-five? Robert Monk and his men are dead.*

Things move quickly after that. Within hours, wagons begin delivering chests of coins and silver bars and Randolph was taken to select our new compound and its mooring spaces.

Five days later, we sailed for Cyprus with nearly one hundred newly released British and other Latin slaves and the coin chests spread around in our various galleys for safekeeping.

We took the priest halfway to Cyprus.

— End of the fifth book —

Please read more. The rest of the action-packed books in this great saga of medieval England are all available on Kindle as eBooks and some are available in print. You can find them by going to your Amazon website and searching for *Martin Archer fiction*. A collection of the first six books is available on Kindle as *The Archers' Story*. Similarly, a collection of the next four novels in the saga is available as *The Archers' Story: Part II,* and there are additional books beyond those four.

I hope you enjoyed reading *The Hostage Archers* as much as I enjoyed writing it. If so, I would respectfully request a favourable review on Amazon and elsewhere with as many stars as possible in order to encourage other readers. I would also value and appreciate your comments. I can reached at martinarcherV@gmail.com

Amazon eBooks in the exciting and action-packed *The Company of Archers* saga:
The Archers
The Archers' Castle
The Archer's War
The Archer's Return
Rescuing the Hostages
Kings and Crusaders
The Archers' Gold
The Missing Treasure
Castling the King
The Sea Warriors
The Captain's Men

Gulling the Kings
The Archers' Magna Carta

Amazon eBooks in Martin Archer's exciting and action-packed *Soldier and Marines* saga:
Soldier and Marines
Peace and Conflict
War Breaks Out
War in the East
Israel's Next War

Collections
The Archer's Story - books I, II, III, IV, V, VI
The Archer's Story II - books VII, VIII, IX, X,
Soldiers and Marines Trilogy

Other eBooks you might enjoy:
Cage's Crew by Martin Archer writing as Raymond Casey
America's Next War by Michael Cameron

Made in the USA
Lexington, KY
01 March 2019